SATIRE
Today

RICHARD HEAGY

SATIRE Today

The Author asserts the moral right to be identified as the author of this work.

ISBN - 13: 978-0-578-43606-7

Published in the United States of America April 1, 2019 by Northfleet Publishers, an imprint of Northfleet Group LLC

The focus of this book is satire, which is presented in various forms, including blogs, articles, spoofs, sketches, plays and other formats. On the one hand, with the exception of events referred to which are established matters of public record, the content of this book is a work of fiction, with names, characters, dialogue, places and incidents portrayed being the product of the author's imagination, used fictitiously or entirely coincidental. On the other hand, there are exceptions to this as the use of satire, ridicule and criticism requires reference to actual historical or current events, public figures and politicians (whose actions and dialogue are entirely fictional), as well as issues concerning governmental and educational institutions, political correctness and other forms of censorship.

PREFACE

It all started when Wikimedia Commons refused to take down a selfie taken by an Indonesian monkey, actually a macaque. British wildlife photographer David Slater claimed that he owned the copyright to the photograph as his camera had been used. However, it appears that the macaque somehow got hold of the camera and took a now famous self-portrait ("selfie") baring his two large front teeth. Wikimedia refused Slater's take-down request and claimed that no one owns the copyright. This led to numerous articles by lawyers and others about the applicability of copyright laws (primarily those of the United States) to selfies (photographs) taken by monkeys and other animals. Not to be left out, PETA (People for the Ethical Treatment of Animals) added its two-bits by filing a lawsuit against the British photographer (David Slater) in San Francisco for damages on behalf of the monkey (dubbed 'Naruto'), claiming that Naruto owns the copyright to the selfie and requesting that the Court appoint PETA to administer all proceeds from the photos for the benefit of Naruto, his family and his community.

The Author decided to write an article much more comprehensive than those scattered about the internet, including coverage of Indonesian and United Kingdom copyright laws. Considering the topic—a frivolous lawsuit filed on behalf of a monkey on the other side of the world—it became obvious that the article though heavy on copyright law should be in the form of satire.

ENOUGH ABOUT MONKEY SELFIES is rather lengthy, and should be read before the three articles that follow for a better understanding of copyright law.

INTRODUCTION

Satire has been around since the days of Aristophanes in ancient Greece. The goal of this book is to bring readers original content concerning topics not covered by other writers of satire or providing a different perspective.

People's concerns today include jobs, the economy, government spending, health care, climate change, national security, immigration, poverty, or why they lost the last election, to name a few. The world in certain areas is full of shortages: water, food, housing, jobs, medicine and healthcare.

Has anyone not noticed that what is lacking most of all in today's world is humor? This may be the result of some global vitamin deficiency, or more likely, political correctness spreading much as an unstoppable virus or plague released from Pandora's jar, which has now morphed into so-called safe spaces. Hearing, seeing or expressing anything the least bit offensive to one or more persons on the planet is not acceptable in many circles.

It you are thin skinned and easily offended (even if you are not sure why), you might follow the example of the ostrich and put your head in the sand, a safe space where you will not hear words or ideas that might upset you or give you a headache or a rash. For the rest of you, open the book and start reading. If you opened this book by mistake and saw something that offended you, take two euphemisms with a glass of water and lie down for half an hour.

"Political correctness is tyranny with manners"
\- Charlton Heston

DISCLAIMER

Some of the content in this book may contain specific or general information on various legal topics, laws, litigation, or court cases, including analysis of the foregoing. Any such legal information or analysis may be incorrect, inaccurate, incomplete, misleading, non-current when published, or no longer good law; it is provided without any representations or warranties, express or implied, and with no obligation to provide a follow-up on any subsequent legal or other developments. In addition, you should note that the application and impact of relevant laws will vary from jurisdiction to jurisdiction and may change from time to time.

The author shall have no responsibility or liability for any damages resulting from reliance on or use of any information contained in this book. Keep in mind that the purpose of this book is to provide entertainment in the form of satire, and not as an alternative to legal or other advice from your attorney, solicitor or other professional advisor. You should seek advice from a qualified legal or other professional with respect to specific situations. In addition, the author has no responsibility for the accuracy of URLs for external or third-party websites referred to in this book, and does not guarantee that any content on such websites is, or will remain, accurate or appropriate.

Most of the satires previously appeared online in a blog entitled "satire and more", though they have been revised or updated for this book. The website "satireandmore.com" was taken down after interference from hackers the second time, curiously enough a few months after publication of *GET THE PRESIDENT—DOJ Black Book.*

CONTENTS

A POT TO PISS IN – an Interview with Bernie

BERNIE: Well, young man, I am very glad you came out to hear me today.

(He reaches out and shakes the YOUNG MAN's hand)

YOUNG MAN: I didn't have nothin' else to do. All they got on TV right now is reruns.

BERNIE: Nevertheless, I am glad you came.

YOUNG MAN: Whatever!

(Looks at his watch)

BERNIE: You are not in a hurry to get back to work, are you?

YOUNG MAN: No. I got laid off at the factory

BERNIE (looking sympathetic): I am sorry to hear that.

YOUNG MAN: It was a crappy job anyway.

BERNIE: Long hours, minimum wage, and no benefits I suppose.

YOUNG MAN: Yeah, but it don't matter. The owner just up and closed the factory.

BERNIE: How much notice did you get?

YOUNG MAN: None. We all showed up at the factory yesterday morning and found a padlock on the gate.

BERNIE (a look of disbelief): That's it?

YOUNG MAN: No. There was a cardboard sign: "Moved to Mexico."

BERNIE (pointing his finger and shaking his hand): That is what I have been talking about—moving manufacturing jobs out of the U.S.

YOUNG MAN: That's not it.

BERNIE (vigorously): You know who is to blame, of course, Wall Street.

YOUNG MAN: No, it's the owner.

BERNIE (wagging his finger back and forth in disagreement): Nonsense; I tell you it is Wall Street.

YOUNG MAN: You don't understand.

BERNIE (holding up a finger): Oh, but I do young man. Everything is Wall Street's fault.

YOUNG MAN: You've got it all wrong.

BERNIE: Well, almost everything is Wall Street's fault.

YOUNG MAN: They didn't move the factory to Mexico.

BERNIE (puzzled): I thought you said they did.

YOUNG MAN: No. The owner closed the factory and he moved to Mexico.

BERNIE: Where did he move the factory?

YOUNG MAN: He didn't. He just closed it and took off with the foreman's wife to Mexico. I guess it's cheaper to live there.

BERNIE (shrugs): You see; it's still Wall Street's fault.

YOUNG MAN: If you say so.

BERNIE (looking eager): Are you registered to vote?

YOUNG MAN: Yes. I'm an independent.

BERNIE (rubbing his hands together): Excellent.

YOUNG MAN: Just like my dad.

BERNIE (to himself): Looks like another vote.

YOUNG MAN: And my grandfather.

BERNIE: He still votes?

YOUNG MAN: Yes.

BERNIE (sincerely, nodding his head): Admirable. How old is he?

YOUNG MAN: Oh, he died about five years ago.

BERNIE: Did I hear you correctly?

YOUNG MAN: Lots of dead people still vote in this county.

BERNIE: I hope no one continues to collect their Social Security benefits.

YOUNG MAN: Wouldn't surprise me.

BERNIE (looking serious): Young man, what can I do to convince you to vote for me?

YOUNG MAN: Well, I don't know.

BERNIE (hopefully): Free college?

YOUNG MAN: No thanks. You still got to study and it gives me headaches.

BERNIE (frowning): Maybe you would prefer a trade school.

YOUNG MAN: Sounds like too much work.

BERNIE: Do you need free housing?

YOUNG MAN: I live with my dad.

BERNIE (thoughtful): Do you smoke? Maybe you are in favor of relaxing the regulation of certain …

YOUNG MAN: Whoa there. I don't smoke nothin'. If I did, my old man would kick me clear across the river and into the next county.

BERNIE (again, hopefully): What about health insurance?

YOUNG MAN: My dad is a veterinarian. He fixes me up when I get sick.

BERNIE (puzzled): Is there anything you need?

YOUNG MAN: Just a pot to piss in.

BERNIE: You don't have one?

YOUNG MAN: No. We live outside of town and have to use the outhouse behind our home.

BERNIE (pointing his finger and shaking it vigorously): That's unacceptable. Every American (without exception) should have a pot to piss in, and maybe a choice of colors. Even in Russia and China, everyone has a pot to piss in.

YOUNG MAN: It's real inconvenient, especially in the wintertime when it's freezing cold.

BERNIE: Let me get this straight; all you need from your government is a pot to piss in?

YOUNG MAN: Well no, maybe one more thing.

BERNIE (wondering): What would that be?

YOUNG MAN: A six-pack of beer, couple of times a week.

BERNIE (thoughtfully, holding his hands up palms forward): A little unusual, but socialism aims to take care of the needs of all, whatever they may be, from the cradle to the voting booth—I mean the grave.

YOUNG MAN: Is this gonna be free?

BERNIE: Absolutely—free is a synonym for socialism.

YOUNG MAN: What's a synonym?

BERNIE (seriously): A free college education might do you some good. Are you sure that you don't want to reconsider?

YOUNG MAN: No thank you.

BERNIE (holding his hands out, palms up): If you say so.

YOUNG MAN: Who's gonna pay for my piss pot and my beer?

BERNIE: The greedy bastards in the top 1%.

YOUNG MAN: You mean those Wall Street dudes?

BERNIE: Absolutely.

YOUNG MAN: That's great.

BERNIE (enthusiastically): Then, I can count on your vote?

YOUNG MAN: Sure thing.

BERNIE: What about your father?

YOUNG MAN: Will we each get our own pot?

BERNIE: Absolutely.

YOUNG MAN: No problem once I tell my dad we don't have to piss in the outhouse no more.

BERNIE: Great.

YOUNG MAN: Would you also like my grandfather's vote?

BERNIE: Thanks, but that is not really necessary.

<u>THE END</u>

ZOMBIE TECH AWARD – for the iPhone

It is a sunny day, and a line of people of all shapes and sizes wait on the steps of an endless stairway that winds its way upward; all ages and ethnic groups are included. At the top of the stairs is a man (CONCIERGE) who looks about forty years old with a short white beard standing behind a lectern. He is wearing a black tuxedo and sandals with no socks.

CONCIERGE: Next.

(Down the line, a man wearing a long-sleeved turtleneck, blue jeans and sneakers counts the number of people in front of him, about twenty or so; then looks back at the hundreds behind him. He stands in line impatiently and looks at his wrist, having forgotten that he is not wearing a watch. His name is JOBS, or at least it used to be when he was alive. In front of him is a young person wearing a pizza delivery hat (PIZZA GUY) and an "I Love New York" T-shirt; he carries a small black umbrella, but he is nevertheless wet)

USHER (to PIZZA GUY): Here you are, sir. Just fill it out and I will pick it up when you are ready.

(Up and down the line are ushers, all dressed in white togas, handing out questionnaires mounted on clipboards with ballpoint pens. The PIZZA GUY puts his umbrella on the step ahead of him so his hands will be free to fill out the form. The USHER next hands a clipboard and a pen to JOBS)

JOBS: What's this for?

USHER: All applicants have to fill them out.

JOBS: Applicants?

USHER: You don't think just anyone can walk through the Pearly Gates, do you?

(JOBS grudgingly takes the clipboard and glances over the questions, then attempts to return it to the USHER)

JOBS: Why should I fill this out? You already know everything about me.

USHER: Yes, but we like to see if people are lying.

JOBS: It's a waste of time.

USHER: Time is something we have an endless supply of here.

(Some clouds come drifting overhead, followed by raindrops)

PIZZA GUY (to JOBS): Hey, buddy, you want to buy my umbrella?

JOBS (to the USHER): I didn't know you had rain up here.

USHER: On occasion, a cloud finds its way up here, but you will not need an umbrella. Even if some rain falls on you, you will remain dry.

JOBS (pointing to the step above him): What about him?

USHER: Oh, he was wet when he arrived, so he will stay wet for the duration of his stay.

JOBS: He might get sick.

USHER: No, his condition will remain the same as when he arrived.

(The PIZZA GUY takes out a cigarette and places it between his lips, searches unsuccessfully in his pockets for a match, then motions to the USHER)

PIZZA GUY: Hey, buddy, you got a light?

USHER: Smoking is not allowed here.

PIZZA GUY: Where's the sign says so?

USHER: There is no place to put a sign.

(The PIZZA GUY tosses his cigarette away, and it lands nearby, suspended in the air)

USHER: No littering.

(The USHER retrieves the cigarette and hands it to the PIZZA GUY, who puts it in his pocket. The PIZZA GUY starts to say something, but the USHER cuts him off)

USHER: I know; there's no sign.

(JOBS starts to fill out the questionnaire, but the pen will not work. He shakes it, tries again, then hands it back to the USHER)

USHER: I will be right back as soon as I find another pen.

(The USHER leaves and someone suddenly appears out of nowhere)

DEVIL: Psst—would you mind stepping over here for a minute?

JOBS: How am I going to do that? There's nothing to stand on if I get off the stairs.

DEVIL: Not at all, sir, you will be standing on air.

JOBS: Why should I believe you?

DEVIL: Look at me; there's nothing underneath my feet.

JOBS: So I see, but I don't want to lose my place in line.

(The line is moving forward slowly as all this takes place)

DEVIL: I'll see to it that you don't.

JOBS: Who are you anyway?

DEVIL: An usher, but not just any usher.

JOBS: You are not dressed the same; well, maybe you are, except that your clothes are off white, even kind of soiled looking.

DEVIL: Step over here. I want to have a little chat with you.

(They move away from the stairs, far enough for the others not to overhear. JOBS looks down nervously as he walks on the air)

JOBS: Are you trying to solicit a bribe to ease my way through the Pearly Gates?

DEVIL: Nothing of the kind. Getting you through the Pearly Gates is last thing I would ever want to do.

JOBS: By the way, who is that man behind the pedestal? I thought St. Peter was supposed to admit people.

DEVIL: He's the CONCIERGE. They are trying to upgrade the place to improve their ratings.

(JOBS glances at his wrist, forgetting again that his watch is not there)

JOBS: How long have I been in line?

DEVIL: Three days.

JOBS: Three days? That's impossible.

DEVIL: You will never experience time again, only eternity.

JOBS: Who are you?

DEVIL: I have been known by many names—Lucifer, Beelzebub, Satan, or more commonly the Devil. I prefer Prince of Darkness myself.

JOBS: I have been called many names myself.

DEVIL: Yes—tyrant, genius and jerk, to name a few.

JOBS: How do I know that you are the devil?

DEVIL: What if I perform a miracle before your very eyes?

JOBS: OK, try me.

(The DEVIL waves his hand in the air and instantly he is holding a deck of cards, which he fans)

DEVIL: Pick a card, any card.

JOBS: That is a cheap card trick, not a miracle.

DEVIL: I don't want to draw attention to myself this close to the Pearly Gates; I can't do anything splashy. Go on, pick a card.

(JOBS takes a card)

JOBS: Now what?

DEVIL: Put it back in the deck.

(The devil shuffles the deck and holds it in the palm of his hand)

DEVIL: Turn over the top card.

(JOBS turns over the top card and holds it up, showing a three of clubs)

DEVIL: What did I tell you?

JOBS: It's not my card.

DEVIL: Are you sure?

JOBS: It is not my card; I had a seven of diamonds.

DEVIL: I must be out of practice.

JOBS: Assuming that you are the devil, why are you here—to tempt me?

DEVIL: Not at all.

JOBS: What do you want?

DEVIL: I want to thank you.

JOBS: For what? I have led an exemplary life, no bad habits of any significance that come to mind.

DEVIL: Results are what count, not the intention to do bad things.

JOBS: I have no idea what you are talking about.

DEVIL: Let's take the iPhone, for example.

JOBS: What about it?

DEVIL: First, let's clear up something. Who invented the iPhone?

JOBS: I did. Everyone knows that.

DEVIL: Not everyone. Some Congresswoman said the government invented the iPhone, not you or Apple.

JOBS: Sour grapes.

DEVIL: Sour grapes invented the iPhone instead of you?

JOBS: That's not what I meant.

DEVIL: Then you take full credit for its invention.

JOBS: Absolutely. Just because engineers were working under my direction does not make me any less the inventor.

DEVIL: Thank God—oops—I shouldn't use that expression. Then I didn't come all this way for nothing. I suppose you consider the iPhone to be the greatest benefit to humanity in modern times.

JOBS: It's the best thing since sliced bread.

DEVIL: Not a good example; bread contains gluten and other unhealthy ingredients.

JOBS: It's just an expression, not a comparison. The iPhone has brought people closer together all around the world, made communications easier and improved their lives.

DEVIL: What about the negatives?

JOBS: I can't think of any, although some people complain about the price.

DEVIL: First, you have not made communication and interaction between people better, aside from a technical standpoint. Communication online is faceless; many hours are wasted each day by exchanging meaningless twaddle. For example, what is the importance of letting all of the people you are deluded into thinking are your friends know that you are spending the weekend cleaning out your closet.

JOBS: Not everyone spends the weekend cleaning out closets.

DEVIL: They spend the rest of the weekend telling their friends, and I use the term friends loosely, how they are wasting their time.

JOBS: Why are we talking about this?

DEVIL: Look what you are doing to education.

JOBS: Increasing educational levels by making more information available.

DEVIL: Hogwash. Everyone is texting; no one knows how to write a complete sentence anymore, not even a short one.

JOBS: Everyone is too busy these days.

DEVIL: Busy doing what? Nothing of any great importance as far as I can tell.

JOBS: One of the biggest benefits to people is mobility, the ability to communicate with friends and business associates, shop and do other things from anywhere, twenty-four hours a day.

DEVIL: Your award may be posthumous, but it is never too late to give recognition to one deserving it.

JOBS: Are you giving me an award?

DEVIL: Almost everyone with an iPhone uses it while walking, wherever he or she is, crossing the street through traffic, riding a bicycle, skate boarding or even texting while driving.

JOBS: It is convenient.

DEVIL: You idiot. People walk into each other and cause automobile accidents while texting. Just look at how many people in line behind you are talking on their mobile phones or trying to send text messages.

JOBS (looking pleased): I am surprised it works up here.

DEVIL: Actually it doesn't. Those fools talking in line were on their mobile phones when they died. They continue as if nothing has happened and don't realize that their conversations and text messages are not going anywhere and that no one is listening or responding. You have created an entire world of self-centered zombies, something I could never do. That is why you have earned the Devil's Award for Outstanding Achievement—for disservice to humanity. This year we are naming it the Zombie Tech Award in your honor.

JOBS: What if I don't want it.

DEVIL: It's too late. The award is all over the internet and available on every iPhone as we speak.

JOBS: Take it down.

DEVIL: Impossible. You have made your technology so secure that even I cannot break into it.

(The line moves up as JOBS and the DEVIL talk. JOBS then returns to the line and tries to squeeze back in between the PIZZA GUY with the umbrella, now number one in the line, and the woman who was previously behind JOBS)

WOMAN: What do you think you are doing?

JOBS: Reclaiming my place in line.

WOMAN: Buzz off, bozo. The back of the line is that way, at the bottom of the stairs.

DEVIL: Madam, this gentleman …

WOMAN: Who is this, your brother? You both have the same eyebrows and piercing eyes.

JOBS: You don't want to know who he is.

WOMAN (pondering): I recognize you now. You are the big cheese who fired me on the spot in front of my co-workers and yelled obscenities at me.

JOBS: I don't recall the situation, but you are not the only one that I fired in person.

(JOBS has worked his way in front of the woman and is now first in line)

CONCIERGE: Next.

(The USHER takes the questionnaire from JOBS and looks at it)

USHER (to the CONCIERGE): He didn't fill it out completely.

CONCIERGE: Send him back to the end of the line.

(The USHER hands the questionnaire back to JOBS and points down the stairs)

CONCIERGE: Next.

THE END

BREXIT – Cameron Thank You Dinner for Obama

The UK Prime Minister and the US President sit at a table in the far corner of a small upscale restaurant in Mayfair on a quiet street in London; nearby, but out of sight, are several secret service agents and security guards. The WAITER approaches the table and asks what they would like to drink.

CAMERON: Whiskey.

OBAMA: Beer.

WAITER: I am sorry sir, but we no longer serve beer. Perhaps you would like something from the bar or maybe a glass of wine.

OBAMA: Wine will be fine.

CAMERON: I will have wine also; cancel the whiskey.

WAITER: Very good, sir, I will send over the sommelier.

(OBAMA and CAMERON listen to the sommelier's suggestions and finally agree on one)

OBAMA: I brought you a present.

CAMERON: How nice. I hope it did not cost too much.

OBAMA: Not at all, but it is one of your favorites; at least that is what they said on the news.

(OBAMA hands a nicely wrapped box to CAMERON, who holds up the box and shakes it. Something inside makes a noise and the contents shift a bit)

OBAMA: You will never guess what it is; might as well just open it.

CAMERON: You are probably right.

OBAMA: I am always right. It comes with being a Harvard law professor; no one questions you until you go into politics.

(CAMERON carefully tears off the wrapping and opens the box; then pulls out the gift—a tube of Pringles)

OBAMA (smiling): They are Paprika Pringles.

CAMERON: How did you know I liked these?

OBAMA: There was a video of you on the internet; you were on a budget flight eating Paprika Pringles.

CAMERON: How thoughtful.

OBAMA: Oh, I really cannot take all the credit, maybe most of it. You know how so many gifts are not what somebody wants at all. I had a White House intern do a search to find out what you really like—here it is.

CAMERON: I do not know what to say, except thanks.

(He opens the tube, inhales, takes one out and tastes it)

CAMERON (to OBAMA): Would you like to try one?

(Before OBAMA can respond, a WAITER walks over to the table)

WAITER: Excuse me sir, I mean Prime Minister, but you may not bring food into the restaurant.

(The WAITER reaches out and snatches the tube of Pringles from CAMERON, but unnoticed by either of them a SECRET SERVICE AGENT appears from nowhere, turns the WAITER round and butts him in the head. The tube falls on the table and the Pringles scatter on the floor)

OBAMA: I brought those all the way from Washington.

OBAMA (to SECRET SERVICE AGENT): Pick those up.

SECRET SERVICE AGENT: Yes, sir.

(The SECRET SERVICE AGENT squats, picks up the Pringles one by one, and blows the dirt off them before putting them back in the tube)

OBAMA: It is hard to get good help these days, even if you are the President of the United States.

(Blood drips from the forehead of the WAITER onto his crisply starched white shirt as he holds his head in pain. The MAÎTRE D' rushes over and helps the WAITER walk away)

CAMERON: Tell me about it. Good help is also hard to find here.

(ANOTHER WAITER arrives with the drinks, followed by the MAÎTRE D', who serves the starters enclosed in silver covers)

MAÎTRE D': Compliments of the chef, in honor of the American President.

(He uncovers the dishes to reveal a surprise)

CAMERON: Seems to be a tiny square hamburger.

OBAMA: It looks like a White Castle.

(He takes a bite and smiles at the MAÎTRE D')

OBAMA (continuing): Please give my thanks to the chef.

(Dinner continues with a salad, bread with a plate of olive oil, followed by the main course, all of which takes a few hours)

CAMERON: Had enough to eat?

OBAMA: It is probably enough to last all week. I should walk it off in Hyde Park in the morning, but my secret service agents will probably complain—always telling me what I can't do.

(As CAMERON and OBAMA are enjoying after dinner drinks, the WAITER returns to the table with several bandages on his forehead)

OBAMA: I am sorry about what happened. I was beginning to get worried—it took you so long.

WAITER: First, I called the nearest hospital emergency room and asked for an ambulance. When I described my injuries, they said it was not serious enough for an ambulance, and suggested that I take a taxi.

OBAMA: Looks like they fixed you up. Your socialized medicine is excellent, so I hear.

WAITER: Where did you hear that?

OBAMA: Uh …

WAITER: I waited in a large room full of tired and angry people, some coughing and sneezing, for four hours; no it was 3 hours and 48 minutes, as they must release you in 4 hours.

OBAMA: Well, anyway the exam must have been thorough.

WAITER: What exam? They dabbed my forehead with some stinging substance, slapped on three small bandages, and gave me two paracetamol—what you would call aspirin.

OBAMA: Again, I am very sorry about what happened. You should go home and get some rest.

(The WAITER nods and leaves)

CAMERON: I invited you here to express my appreciation for your support with the EU referendum, especially your recommendation that the United Kingdom stay in the European Union.

OBAMA: Remaining in the EU gives the UK more influence and is important for economic prosperity and security. It is most unfortunate that the Leave vote prevailed.

CAMERON: I should have never authorized the referendum. The Leave vote has been a shock to everyone, even the Leave supporters. The financial markets are in disarray and the pound is in the toilet.

(A tall stocky man with unruly blonde hair, much like a miniature haystack, approaches the table and pulls out a chair. He is BORIS JOHNSON, former Mayor of London and now a Member of Parliament)

BORIS (as he sits down): May I join you?

CAMERON: Looks like you already have.

OBAMA: I thought that the referendum was primarily about the economy and security, but it seems that immigration became a more significant factor as the vote neared.

BORIS: Maybe so, but substantial support for the Leave vote already existed for other important reasons. This is also about representative democracy. Unelected faceless EU civil servants impose endless rules, regulations and financial obligations on the UK. The press and the elite have neglected the obstacles the EU has created for business, especially small shopkeepers, as well as unduly interfering with the daily private lives of ordinary people with petty overregulation. The European Court of Justice overrules English laws and judges, something the US would never stand for, as evidenced by their refusing to recognize the jurisdiction of the International Court of Justice.

CAMERON: I did negotiate with the EU and got them to agree to some changes in our favor.

BORIS (to CAMERON): I know you tried your best, but you really did not get much. The bloated EU bureaucracy is extremely inflexible from top to bottom, starting with European Commission President Jean-Claude Juncker. He is so rigid that I would not be surprised if he could not even bend over to tie his shoelaces. The man has this ever-closer phobia and keeps pushing the EU down a one-way road to failure. What started as an economic union—with the European Economic Community in 1975—morphed into the European Union in 1993, a political union with an insatiable hunger for fiscal, diplomatic and unchecked legislative powers.

(Although OBAMA finished his dinner some time ago, a small piece of bread remains on the table. He picks it up and dips it in a small plate of olive oil)

BORIS (to OBAMA): It is much healthier to dip bread in olive oil than to smoother it with butter, do you not agree?

OBAMA: I believe everyone knows that.

BORIS: Dip away while you can. In 2014, the EU tried to ban the use of refillable bottles and dipping bowls of olive oil at restaurant tables. There was an unusual groundswell against the proposal across Europe by consumers and restaurant owners. It was one of the very few times that the EU backed down and reversed one of its rules, never admitting it was wrong, but excusing itself by saying that the ban was not formulated so as to achieve wide support from the public, as if the EU has ever given a rat's ass about public opinion. They always know better and want to impose their way of thinking by re-educating the public, a common trait of those in unelected positions. I would not be surprised if they tried something like this again; the UK will still be subject to EU regulations until they negotiate the terms of withdrawal from the EU and it becomes final.

A NEW WAITER (arrives out of nowhere, pushing a cart): Gentlemen, I have the pleasure of preparing Bananas Foster at your table.

(The cart contains a large skillet on an alcohol burner, brown sugar, butter, rum, banana liquor, and several bananas)

OBAMA: I have not eaten Bananas Foster for quite some time.

(An elderly man—the MINDER—with white hair, a face with more wrinkles than his worn, ill-fitting soviet era brown suit, and a short military-style haircut suddenly appears and pulls out a small tool—a digital angle finder, picks up a banana and measures its curvature or bend. He speaks with an East German accent)

MINDER (to NEW WAITER): You will take these bananas back immediately; their bend violates EU regulations.

(The MINDER puts the banana back on the cart and NEW WAITER pushes the cart away)

CAMERON: I thought that the bend rules applied to cucumbers.

BORIS: Yes, but it is more complicated for cucumbers than bananas because there are two cucumber categories. Class I cucumbers allow a bend of 10mm per 10cm of length, whereas Class II cumbers can bend twice as much.

CAMERON: Wait a minute. I think the rule on bananas was eliminated in the UK a few years back.

MINDER: Nobody told me. I will have to fill out a report concerning this violation.

(He takes out a pad of forms and makes notations on the top one)

MINDER: Your names.

CAMERON: I am the Prime Minister of the United Kingdom.

MINDER: And I am the King of Bavaria.

BORIS: He really is the Prime Minister.

BORIS and OBAMA (to themselves): Not for long.

MINDER: And, I suppose you are the Mayor of London

(pause)

MINDER (continuing): For the pittance they pay me, I am not going to verify your names. I just need to write something in each blank on this form so none of the highly paid comrades in Brussels sends it back.

(He starts filling out the form and turns to OBAMA)

MINDER (to OBAMA): Don't think I have forgotten about you. You look like a university professor. I'll just write *professor*, since you gentlemen are playing games with me about your real names. They don't matter because the guilty party subject to a fine is the restaurant.

OBAMA: That's OK; I can get some Bananas Foster next time I am in New Orleans.

(OBAMA picks up a thin briefcase and pulls out a group of articles that mention Cameron and the EU referendum. He holds them out to CAMERON, but the MINDER grabs them and pulls off the large paperclip holding them together)

MINDER: What have we here?

BORIS: Now what?

OBAMA: The articles are not all negative.

BORIS: That is not the problem; it is the petty EU bureaucracy.

(The MINDER pulls out a small ruler and measures the length of the paper clip)

MINDER: Just as I suspected; this clip exceeds the allowable size under EU regulations.

(He bends the paperclip and it snaps in two)

MINDER: Oh, my, look at this. This clip appears to be made of materials that violate EU safety regulations. I'll have to confiscate it and write another report.

(The Minder drops the unclipped papers on the table, fills out another form and departs. Before he leaves, he clicks his heels together and raises his right arm in a Nazi salute)

MINDER: Sorry. Old habits are hard to break.

OBAMA: First it's bananas; now paper clips.

(He straightens the papers and hands them to CAMERON)

CAMERON: Thank you. I am sure I will find them interesting.

OBAMA: Who was that fellow?

BORIS: A minder.

OBAMA: Did you say a miner?

BORIS: No, a minder—one of those low-level officials assigned to follow you around if you visited Soviet controlled countries in the old days. They would stick to you like glue.

OBAMA: I thought that all went out with the end of the Cold War.

CAMERON: It is just something the EU is trying on a temporary basis.

BORIS: There is no such thing as temporary where the EU is concerned. They will make this so-called experiment permanent and expand it.

OBAMA: Why was that fellow measuring the bananas?

CAMERON: The EU wants to ensure that its rules and regulations are being followed. They have placed staff members in a few restaurants on a test basis to oversee compliance in the food service industry.

BORIS: Staff members, bloody hell. These are former minders from East Germany here to spy on us for the EU; a relic from the Cold War, straight out of Alexanderplatz central casting in Berlin. They are state employees who cannot be retrained for other jobs. An invasive program our Prime Minister has allowed into the UK.

CAMERON: I saw his resume—he comes with a recommendation, somewhat dated, from Erich Honecker.

BORIS: Wonderful fellow as far as apparatchiks go, especially known for organizing the building of the Berlin Wall.

OBAMA (to himself): I wonder if Donald Trump has heard of him?

CAMERON: Don't blame me; the UK has to follow the EU directives or they raise a big stink or take legal action.

BORIS (to OBAMA): You probably thought the EU referendum was just about security and the economy.

OBAMA: Well yes. That is what first comes to mind.

BORIS: The problem that mostly affects the daily lives of UK citizens is the constant generation of new regulations, most of them quite petty. Job security is sacred at the European Commission. It is almost impossible to be fired, but people still like to give the appearance of being busy. I would not be surprised to find that they have classes to teach civil servants how to look busy when they have nothing to do. More than 10,000 EU officials make more than our Prime Minister does. The latest proposal, so I hear, is to offer an incentive system for lower-paid employees who submit three ideas each week for new things to regulate.

OBAMA: There is nothing wrong with big government, but I don't know about that kind of incentive system.

OBAMA (to BORIS): You were a major supporter of the Leave campaign. What are their plans for carrying out the Brexit?

BORIS (ignoring the question): Do you own a dog?

OBAMA: Two.

BORIS: Well, you probably have the same rules as in the UK; you must carry a plastic bag and pick up after your dog makes a deposit.

OBAMA: Yes, but it is not a big inconvenience.

BORIS: You might have a problem with your dogs if you move to London after you leave the White House, at least until we are out of the EU.

OBAMA: I wasn't planning to, but why is that?

BORIS: The EU regulators in their concern for the environment are going all out after plastic.

OBAMA: I see nothing wrong with that.

BORIS: They are considering banning the use of plastic bags for dog walkers.

OBAMA: Then, how are you going to clean up the dog deposits?

BORIS: Dog owners will have to train their dogs to sit on the pot to take a crap before they go for a walk. Quite an inconvenience for dog owners, but it will be good for business.

OBAMA: How is that?

BORIS: They already make special potty seats for small children and disabled persons. Now they will need to design special ones for dogs, and one size fits all will not work. Even so, the solicitors will be concerned about liability if an owner uses the wrong size and a dog falls in and drowns, so more work for them. Potty manufacturers and the owners of pet stores will also benefit from increased sales.

(NEW WAITER appears with the dessert menu and asks to take their orders)

OBAMA: I am not hungry anymore.

CAMERON: Me neither.

BORIS (to NEW WAITER): Bring those bananas back. I'll take them home and make my own Bananas Foster.

NEW WAITER: I am sorry but the MINDER confiscated them.

BORIS: What is he going to do—send them with his report to Brussels?

NEW WAITER: No. I saw him through the window, standing at the bus stop. He was eating the bananas.

THE END

HITLER's ERASURE – EU Article 17
[The Right to be Forgotten]

Someone long thought to be dead recently filed a complaint with the European Commission for violation of his human rights, in particular, the right to be forgotten and erasure of personal data no longer relevant pursuant to Article 17. They wondered if perhaps a relative or descendant filed the complaint. The European Commission, not burdened with budget restraints, dispatched one of its highly paid bureaucrats to the far ends of the globe to investigate the complaint, and in particular verify the identity of the actual complainant. After a flight from Brussels to Buenos Aires, followed by a long train ride and change of buses, the highly paid bureaucrat (unaccustomed to such uncomfortable travel accommodations) arrived at his fact-finding destination in Argentina.

BUS DRIVER: End of the line.

(The bus stops at the corner of a side street that abuts the town plaza and all depart, including a few chickens. The EU OFFICIAL is the last one off the bus. He holds a briefcase in one hand and with the other hand dusts off his jacket; then looks round as everyone disappears. Small shops and cafés line the plaza, accompanied by a few kiosks or food stands here and there. Suddenly, what appears to be a taxi approaches, belching exhaust, comes to a sudden halt)

DRIVER: Señor, at your service.

EU OFFICIAL: Am I supposed to ride in that thing?

DRIVER: The Mercedes is in the shop.

EU OFFICIAL: Naturally.

DRIVER: It's not really in the shop. We rarely use it so as not to attract unwanted attention. I am here to pick you up. He does not trust anyone else.

EU OFFICIAL: Him? Oh, you mean …

DRIVER: Don't say his name in public.

EU OFFICIAL: Of course not.

DRIVER: It's just a short distance.

(They ride to the far side of the plaza and stop by an ice cream stand, which is in front of an empty store. Postcards line the rectangular shape of the stand. The proprietor (ADOLF) is slender with piercing eyes, short and sports a beard that cannot make up its mind if it is grey or black. The same may be said about what little hair remains on the top of his head, revealed when he occasionally takes off his straw hat to fan himself. He sits on a tall stool behind the ice cream containers)

ADOLF (leaning forward): May I help you?

EU OFFICIAL: I am here about your complaint.

ADOLF: Which one?

EU OFFICIAL: Involving the EU.

ADOLF: Did you want some ice cream?

EU OFFICIAL: Not really, I'm lactose intolerant.

ADOLF: This is a small town. People will be suspicious if you stand here without buying something.

EU OFFICIAL: Maybe a chocolate ice cream cone, just one scoop.

ADOLF: We do not have different flavors, just pure white vanilla—with no vanilla bean specks.

EU OFFICIAL: I might have guessed.

(ADOLF places a small scoop of vanilla on a waffle cone and hands it to the EU OFFICIAL)

ADOLF: That will be 25 pesos. Hand me your ID when you give me the money.

(ADOLF examines the front and back of the ID, then returns it)

ADOLF (continuing): How was your trip?

EU OFFICIAL: OK, but first-class was sold out so I had to fly business class from Brussels to Buenos Aires.

ADOLF: We all have to bear life's hardships.

EU OFFICIAL: Then it took ten hours by train to Córdoba.

ADOLF: The bus is more comfortable, but you should have flown; it takes less than two hours.

EU OFFCIAL: What? The travel agent told me there were no flights between Buenos Aires and Córdoba. She obviously sabotaged me because I interrupted her while she was texting a friend about what nail polish to wear.

ADOLF: Unbelievable.

EU OFFICIAL: The bus ride from Córdoba to Villa Maria was comfortable at first and took about two hours. However, the last part—from Villa Maria to here—was terrible. The ride was very bumpy and the bus broke down twice. Each time the bus stopped for repairs, the driver waited for a priest to bless the bus before he would continue.

ADOLF: If you think that was bad, you should have been on the submarine that brought me to Argentina. First, I had to fly to Denmark in a light plane. Then a couple of weeks on a submarine—diving every time there was trouble on the horizon.

EU OFFICIAL: Was that one of those U-530 submarines that surrendered to the Argentine Navy at Mar del Plata in July of 1945?

ADOLF: No, I arrived a week or so later, stayed for a while in Córdoba, then stayed at a couple of ranches outside of Bariloche. There were many Nazis, I mean Germans, living in and around Bariloche at the time, but of course I had to stay out of sight so I could not walk around the city or enjoy the German restaurants.

(He sneezes)

EU OFFICIAL: Gesundheit!

ADOLF: Are you crazy?

EU OFFICIAL: What do you mean?

ADOLF: Do not speak to me in German. Are you trying to get me killed?

EU OFFICIAL: Certainly not.

ADOLF: Even though I avoid going into Bariloche, there are many Germans in the surrounding area and I am always worried that someone might recognize me. Every so often, I feel the need to move on for my safety, so, for now I am here where there are no other Germans.

EU OFFICIAL: By the way, how is it that you are still alive? Everyone thinks you are dead.

ADOLF: As Mark Twain once said, "reports of my death have been greatly exaggerated."

EU OFFICIAL: You must be at least 125 years old by now.

ADOLF: You stop counting after 100. It gets harder and harder to walk with the arthritis reaching more places.

EU OFFICIAL: What is your secret—something you got from Doctor Mengele?

ADOLF: He died almost 30 years ago, and longevity was not his specialty.

EU OFFICIAL: Right—they did call him the *Angel of Death.*

ADOLF: Have you have heard of Doctor Oz?

EU OFFICIAL: Are you referring to the *Wizard of Oz*?

ADOLF: Don't be ridiculous.

EU OFFICIAL: Who is Doctor Oz then?

ADOLF: One of those American television personalities, I believe. They are always promoting vitamin supplements or something or other to improve your health.

EU OFFICIAL: So the secret is vitamins, is it?

ADOLF: I am not sure, but it is probably some combination of herbs. I heard from an American tourist some time ago about this Doctor Oz, who is a real medical doctor, and I looked into it.

EU OFFICIAL: Maybe I can get some of this longevity stuff. It would be great for my career if I could outlast my contemporaries in the EU and rise to the top through attrition.

ADOLF: First, I don't even know the actual name of it. They have to put something innocuous on the label to get through customs, so the label says "Natural Cooking Spices" and lists the ingredients: cumin, turmeric and ginger.

EU OFFICIAL: Maybe I can have a chemist experiment with varying the proportions of the ingredients to replicate the formula.

ADOLF: It's not that simple. My supplier removes the original label and replaces it with a fake; whatever the ingredients are, they are not cumin, turmeric or ginger. Proof is in the odor and the taste.

EU OFFICIAL: You said first; that means there must be a second reason, or maybe more.

ADOLF: Of course there is. If you were to get your hands on a bottle of this stuff or even if you discovered the formula, it would not do you any good in Europe.

EU OFFICIAL: I don't follow you.

ADOLF: You would have to move here for it to work.

EU OFFICIAL: Move here. You must be kidding.

ADOLF: Not at all. The formula only prolongs life because of the local water; something happens when they are mixed together.

EU OFFICIAL: What would I do here?

ADOLF: Maybe raise some goats or weave baskets. I hear it is very relaxing, but I have never tried it myself.

EU OFFICIAL: Let's just forget about it. Is there anything you miss from Germany?

ADOLF: I used to watch Disney animations.

EU OFFICIAL: Mickey Mouse cartoons?

ADOLF: Mickey Mouse was a degenerate tap-dancing idiot. My favorite was *Snow White*; it was actually based on a German fairy tale known as *Sneewittchen*.

EU OFFICIAL: I never knew that.

ADOLF: Maybe we should discuss what you came here for.

EU OFFICIAL: I was about to say that.

ADOLF: First, you might want to wipe the ice cream off your jacket. It's dripping because you are just holding it. You didn't even taste it.

EU OFFICIAL: Shit. Do you have a towel?

(ADOLF looks around, finds a rag and hands it to the EU OFFICIAL, who brushes himself off)

ADOLF: You are lucky it isn't chocolate.

EU OFFICIAL: Why are you selling ice cream? You must have enough money to live comfortably without working.

ADOLF: You people in Brussels must have your heads so far in the clouds you couldn't even hear an elephant fart in the building lobby, if there were one in the lobby. There is probably some EU regulation that prohibits elephants within 500 kilometers from EU buildings even though there are no elephants in Brussels; I wouldn't be surprised if the regulation also applies to ants, not that you could enforce it.

EU OFFICIAL: Well, I am able to recognize that you did not answer my question.

ADOLF: Everyone is required to have an identity card, which must list an address and an occupation.

EU OFFICIAL: Can't you just say you are retired?

ADOLF: Retired from what—Chancellor of Germany, or Führer of the Third Reich?

EU OFFICIAL: I guess not.

ADOLF: This town is not that big. Even if retired were an acceptable category, people would wonder about the source of my income.

(He scoops up some ice cream, puts it in a cone and holds it out to the EU OFFICIAL)

EU OFFICIAL: I don't want another ice cream.

ADOLF: Take it before someone wonders why you are just standing in the hot sun talking to me for such a long time.

(The EU OFFICIAL takes it and reluctantly tastes it)

ADOLF (continuing): There's a fellow across the plaza has a bookshop that stocks international travel books in several languages.

EU OFFICIAL: Looking at the people around here, I find it hard to believe that they have enough money to travel abroad.

ADOLF: Nevertheless, he makes a good living.

EU OFFICIAL: Selling books to locals?

ADOLF: He makes money off tourists. His nephew is a pickpocket.

EU OFFICIAL: Oh.

ADOLF: Now, do you understand? I am an ice cream vendor. I can't just say so, or someone would get suspicious. So, I spend a couple hours a day selling ice cream, to tourists and a few locals. It's the locals I have to be careful with, especially the Comandante de Policía, but he's no problem when he brings his two little girls for an ice cream cone. Ice cream is very popular in Argentina and I always give them a double.

EU OFFICIAL: What's with the postcards?

ADOLF: You must know that when I lived in Vienna I was an artist. I produced hundreds of works, paintings and postcards, mostly watercolors. Now I just paint postcards; the tourists seem to like them and I sell quite a few. Nowadays I just paint local scenes, nothing like my previous work in Germany, as I do not want to be recognized by some visiting art historian. I use watercolors and then convert them to printed postcards. Of course, they are unsigned.

EU OFFICIAL: Most interesting, but back to the matter at hand. You have filed a complaint under EU Article 17 concerning your right to be forgotten and erasure of your personal details on the internet. Regulations create an obligation for a controller, such as Google, who has made personal data public, to ensure erasure of such data where an individual wants his data deleted because it is no longer needed or still relevant.

ADOLF: I know all that.

EU OFFICIAL: Instead of filing a request for deletion with Google or some other data controller, you have filed a complaint directly with the EU, for which there is no such procedure.

ADOLF: That's not the point. The EU by regulation can expand this right to be forgotten and to erasure to all relevant parties. Otherwise, it is a hollow rule because someone's personal information is still widely available on the internet and in print, such as bookstores and even worse, in classrooms.

EU OFFICIAL: What good would such expansion of the regulation do, unless there is some way to enforce it? Do you propose that we burn all of the books that mention you—other than *Mein Kampf*?

ADOLF: No, just the ones that portray me in a bad light.

EU OFFICIAL: I think that would come close to 100%.

ADOLF: You may be right, but all of those things, if they did happen, which I do not admit, were such a long time ago.

EU OFFICIAL: The cost of destroying all history books in the schools and replacing them in Germany alone would be prohibitive for starters.

ADOLF: I have a solution.

EU OFFICIAL: Your last one did not work out so well.

ADOLF: You see, you yourself are an example of why my right to be forgotten and to erasure should be respected; it is a fundamental human right and should apply to everyone.

EU OFFICIAL: But you are an historical figure.

ADOLF: Bah. I hear that they don't even teach history in the schools or universities anymore. Some hogwash about safe spaces, spread by a recent disease called political correctness.

EU OFFICIAL: Maybe so, but that argument is not going to convince anyone in Brussels. Assuming for arguments sake that the cost was not prohibitive, it is not a practical solution as students would not have access to history books until new ones could be printed and distributed.

ADOLF: As I said, I have a solution, one that will not only solve the problem but increase employment for downsized older workers, especially the ones who cannot be trained for newer technological jobs.

EU OFFICIAL (with a look of skepticism): Go on.

ADOLF: First, you order thousands of black markers; that will help the businesses that produce them, which will need to hire more workers.

EU OFFICIAL (raising his eyebrows): OK.

ADOLF: Hire several hundred editors to redact the objectionable material about me, using the black markers. They would have to work in a secure facility and, of course, need to be searched upon entering and leaving the premises.

EU OFFICIAL: Who would decide what is objectionable?

ADOLF: I would, of course.

EU OFFICIAL: The information would be highly confidential. What if it got lost in the mail?

ADOLF: Quite simple. Deliver it to me by courier. Someone such as you could fly to Buenos Aires, first-class naturally, accompanied by a junior courier, who would fly in the back of the plane. You could fly to Córdoba and stay there while your junior courier journeys onward to see me. Córdoba is much like a European city. You can enjoy fine dining while your junior courier enjoys the train ride to this province, and the last stretch by bus.

EU OFFICIAL (positively): Hum.

ADOLF: The redacted copies will be securely protected at all times in a metal briefcase with a combination lock, and chained to the wrist of the courier. In addition to a government issued ID, the courier will prove his bona fides by using a secret handshake.

EU OFFICIAL: I see.

ADOLF: So far, so good, right?

(The EU OFFICIAL just nods)

ADOLF (continuing): Upon approval of the redactions, the EU will hire thousands of workers to delete the objectionable material by hand, using the black markers. You can feed the redacted books back into the educational institutions piecemeal as they are completed, making the process less disruptive.

EU OFFICIAL: What about others, such as libraries?

ADOLF: They will be scattered around a much wider area than the schools and universities. You should probably have the personnel involved in this project wear some kind of uniform for ease of identification, in addition to government issued photo ID.

EU OFFICIAL: Would they use the secret handshake?

ADOLF: Absolutely not, its use must be extremely limited—probably just for the courier who deals with me.

EU OFFICIAL: I was just trying to cover all bases.

ADOLF: Maybe the uniforms should have some kind of logo.

EU OFFICIAL: Good idea. What colour do you think the uniforms should be?

ADOLF: Maybe brown.

EU OFFICIAL: Just what I was thinking.

ADOLF: Excellent.

EU OFFICIAL: On the other hand, UPS uses brown uniforms, and they deliver packages worldwide.

ADOLF: Hum. We will have to think that over.

EU OFFICIAL: That about raps it up. I believe there is a bus leaving in an hour.

ADOLF: Please keep me informed on your progress.

EU OFFICIAL: Of course, if there is nothing else, I will say goodbye.

ADOLF: Before you leave, would you like to buy some postcards?

THE END

CHINESE ANYONE? - Ask Justice Scalia

ISABEL was a nice looking woman in her fifties, until a large beer, delivery truck came out of nowhere, went through a stop sign, and totaled her small car. She was driving on a county road on her way to a schoolhouse, but she could not remember why; all she remembered was the crash. The schoolhouse was serving as a temporary courthouse while the official one was undergoing repairs. Because of a shortage of judges, initial motions on her case (a discrimination lawsuit for failure to hire ISABEL [also referred to as the PLAINTIFF] to teach Chinese, even though she spoke no Chinese) were to be re-scheduled.

Everything seemed cloudy to ISABEL, but slowly it all came into focus. Instead of being in a hospital room, she found herself walking slowly up a stairway that suddenly branched out towards five different entrances, actually arched gates with names above. The two on the left said "UK" and "EU" respectively, the two on the right "US" and "CHINA"; the one in the middle, much larger, said "MAIN ENTRANCE TO HEAVEN."

It suddenly occurred to ISABEL that she was dead; she had died in the car accident. What lousy timing; she had just commenced an important discrimination lawsuit against the city's only school district.

ISABEL (looking around): Where am I?

VOICE (O.S.): What does it look like?

ISABEL: The Pearly Gates.

VOICE (O.S.): He doesn't like people to call it that.

ISABEL: Sorry.

VOICE (O.S.): The proper name is Heaven.

ISABEL: I want to talk to God.

VOICE (O.S.): Walk up to the main entrance.

(ISABEL walks up to the main entrance and finds a short, old man—GEORGE BURNS—smoking a cigar)

ISABEL: You are not God.

GEORGE BURNS: Well, I played God in the movies.

OTHER VOICES (O.S.) – Richard Pryor and Charlton Heston: Me too.

GEORGE BURNS: Ignore them. I played God in two movies. I am George Burns, or I used to be.

(ST. PETER returns from his break and looks at all the gates)

ST. PETER (to GEORGE BURNS): What have you done? Why are there so many gates?

GEORGE BURNS: It is April 1st; God took away my life but not my sense of humor.

(ST. PETER snaps his fingers; there is a loud clap of thunder and the four extra gates disappear)

ISABEL: I have a complaint. It's about my Chinese ...

ST. PETER: I handle admissions, not complaints. Go back down the stairs, exactly 40 steps, and turn left.

(ISABEL cautiously walks down the stairs, counting each step; then sees a path on the left, which she follows until she comes to a counter, which seems to be floating in the air. Behind the counter stands a pious-looking man (MAN) with a long beard and a strong resemblance to Confucius)

MAN (in Mandarin): Help you?

(They converse for a while, ISABEL in English and the MAN in Mandarin, their voices raising as they speak in frustration at their inability to understand each other)

ISABEL (yelling): I did not ask for someone who speaks Chinese. This is about a Chinese language class, but it is a legal matter. Doesn't anyone here speak English?

(An angel—ST. IVES—appears next to the MAN and taps him on the shoulder. The MAN bows and in response ST. IVES nods his head, whereupon the MAN fades from sight)

ST. IVES: I speak English.

ISABEL: What about the Chinese man? I thought everyone in Heaven could speak all languages.

ST. IVES: Only the Saints have that ability.

ISABEL: Who are you?

ST. IVES: I am ST. IVES, the patron Saint of the go legal profession.

ISABEL: I should not be here.

ST. IVES: How many times have I heard that?

ISABEL: I started legal proceedings that involve important issues concerning racial discrimination. I must return to earth, at least long enough to resolve the case.

ST. IVES: This is quite an unusual request.

ISABEL: I think it has happened many times before.

ST. IVES: That is only in the movies. God is the only one who can grant your request.

GEORGE BURNS (O.S.): Did someone call me?

ST. IVES: Another one of your April Fools pranks, I guess.

GEORGE BURNS (O.S.): There is not much else to do up here.

ST. IVES (to ISABEL): I will be right back.

ISABEL: You're going to consult God?

ST. IVES: No, ST. PETER. You have to go through channels up here just like down below.

(ST. IVES leaves for what seems to be a long time, although time is irrelevant in Heaven. ISABEL paces back and forth until ST. IVES returns)

ISABEL: Well?

ST. IVES: You are in luck. This has never happened before, but God is totally against discrimination.

ISABEL: Do you mean I can return?

ST. IVES: Yes.

ISABEL: It is a miracle.

ST. IVES: Miracles are one of God's specialties.

ISABEL: When do I leave?

ST. IVES: As soon as we discuss the terms and conditions.

ISABEL: You sound like a lawyer. Sorry, I forgot.

ST. IVES: You have 48 hours; then you must return. Whatever decision the court makes will be final. You may not stay longer to appeal if you receive an unfavorable decision.

ISABEL: There is a problem with the 48 hours.

ST. IVES: What would that be?

ISABEL: The trial is to be postponed because of a shortage of local judges. Two went to jail last week for corruption and three went on a hunting trip together. The rest have full calendars.

ST. IVES: No problem. We will send someone from here. I have a recent arrival in mind.

ISABEL: Wait; I can't go back looking like this, not after a deadly car crash.

ST. IVES: You will appear just as you were before the accident.

(ST. IVES claps his hands, followed by a loud thunderbolt. ISABEL finds herself in a makeshift courtroom, in reality a school classroom. She looks round and sees several others, all seated in typical classroom chairs with writing tops. They include PLAINTFF's ATTORNEY, DEFENDANT's ATTORNEY, as well as the JANITOR; up front behind a table sits a large man in black robes, the recently deceased JUSTICE SCALIA)

JUSTICE SCALIA: Where is the BAILFF?

DEFENDANT's ATTORNEY: We don't have one.

JUSTICE SCALIA: We cannot proceed without one.

PLAINTIFF's ATTORNEY: Why don't we use the JANITOR.

DEFENDANT's ATTORNEY: I will agree to that. I am sure he has seen enough TV programs to know what to do.

JUSTICE SCALIA: Very well, but we need a gavel.

JANITOR: I think there is one on the wall in the Principal's office; he got it as some kind of award.

(The JANITOR leaves and goes to the principal's office, which is next door. There are sounds of pounding and breaking glass before the JANITOR returns, gavel in hand. He hands it to JUSTICE SCALIA, who places it on the table)

JANITOR: Sorry about the noise, but I had to break the glass case on the wall.

JUSTICE SCALIA (to the JANITOR): I hereby appoint you as BAILIFF of this court. Now, we may proceed.

BAILIFF: All rise. Court is in session.

(JUSTICE SCALIA nods his head to the BAILIFF in approval as the others rise, with some difficulty, from the small sized classroom chairs)

JUSTICE SCALIA: BAILIFF, read the complaint.

BAILIFF: It is kind of long, and has some big words.

JUSTICE SCALIA: Just give us a summary.

(The BAILIFF reads over the complaint quickly)

BAILIFF: PLAINTIFF has filed a discrimination suit against the DEFENDANT for failure to hire her for some Chinese job; all the other applicants are all Chinese persons.

JUSTICE SCALIA (to PLAINTIFF's ATTORNEY): Counsellor, you may make your opening statement.

(PLAINTIFF's ATTORNEY is young and has been a member of the bar for just over a year. The lighting is poor in the room, and as he approaches the bench, he recognizes the famous justice, but then he is unsure)

PLAINTIFF's ATTORNEY: Is that really you? I just returned from being abroad for eight months and I heard that you had died. I have not seen any mention of you in the local papers since I returned. I guess rumors of your death are premature—just like Mark Twain.

JUSTICE SCALIA: Well, here I am, acting as a circuit judge. Please proceed.

PLAINTIFF's ATTORNEY: PLAINTIFF's suit alleges employment discrimination based on race. She is white and all of the other applicants are Chinese.

JUSTICE SCALIA: Does this involve a Chinese restaurant?

PLAINTIFF's ATTORNEY: No. I am afraid the BAILIFF's summary of the complaint was too brief. PLAINTIFF is suing the DEFENDANT school district for failing to hire her to teach classes in Chinese; I mean Mandarin. As the BAILIFF stated, the PLAINTIFF is white and the other applicants are all Chinese.

JUSTICE SCALIA: Is that it?

PLAINTIFF's ATTORNEY: This community has a large number of companies of various sizes that import products made in China to their specifications. Several of their employees need to learn Chinese. The DEFENDANT offers adult education classes, mostly at night, including Chinese, or more specifically Mandarin. All applicants are required to teach a minimum of two classes per week. There are only two unfilled positions; PLAINTIFF can teach the one in English and have someone else teach the Chinese class for her.

JUSTICE SCALIA: What damages are you seeking?

PLAINTIFF's ATTORNEY: In addition to a job, she is seeking damages for emotional distress, suffering, inconvenience, mental anguish and loss of enjoyment of life.

JUSTICE SCALIA (to DEFENDANT's ATTORNEY): Counsellor, you may present your defense.

DEFENDANT's ATTORNEY: The school district has a clear rule, applied to all persons equally: you must teach a minimum of two classes. PLAINTIFF works fulltime during the day and is only available to teach adult education classes at night. There are only two unfilled evening positions at this time: How to Write a Short Story, which PLAINTIFF is qualified to teach, and Mandarin, which she is not. Failure to hire PLAINTIFF has nothing to do with race.

JUSTICE SCALIA: Who are these other potential applicants?

DEFENDANT's ATTORNEY: Chinese suppliers to some of our local companies have sent a few employees here to learn technology. They are also well educated and qualified to teach Mandarin, it being their native language. Employment is based on knowledge of Mandarin, not race or nationality.

PLAINTIFF's ATTORNEY: Aren't they also supposed to teach two classes, or are you making an exception for them—further discrimination.

DEFENDANT's ATTORNEY: Some of them are also teaching Chinese cooking.

PLAINTIFF's ATTORNEY: Oh.

DEFENDANT's ATTORNEY: PLAINTIFF's complaint fails to state a cause of action with respect to inconvenience and loss of enjoyment of life. Furthermore, we will introduce evidence to show that the latter claim is false and that the PLAINTIFF suffers no emotional distress or mental anguish.

JUSTICE SCALIA (to PLAINTIFF's ATTORNEY): Counsellor, are you telling me that the PLAINTIFF does not speak Chinese; I mean Mandarin.

PLAINTIFF's ATTORNEY: Yes, but she is willing to learn and has already started. I have a witness who will testify as to her progress. Let me make a call and he will be here in 15 minutes or less.

(They take a break until there is a knock on the door and a Chinese man enters with several bags of Chinese food)

JUSTICE SCALIA: What is this? I would have preferred Italian food.

PLAINTIFF's ATTORNEY: This is my witness, the owner (OWNER) of a Chinese restaurant nearby.

(JUSTICE SCALIA decides that they might as well eat before the witness testifies. When they finish, the OWNER is sworn in by the BAILIFF)

PLAINTIFF's ATTORNEY: If the court decides that PLAINTIFF must teach the Mandarin class herself, then, as I have already stated, PLAINTIFF is willing to learn Mandarin, and has already started. She eats Chinese food several times a week and always asks for a handful of extra fortune cookies so that she can learn new words.

JUSTICE SCALIA: Did you say that the PLAINTIFF is learning Mandarin from fortune cookies?

PLAINTIFF's ATTORNEY: Yes, and I will present testimony as to her progress.

DEFENDANT's ATTORNEY (to JUSTICE SCALIA): I believe last year in *Obergefell vs Hodges* you referred to the level of wisdom delivered to diners at the end of a Chinese meal. Your dissenting opinion stated, in part, "The Supreme Court of the United States has descended from the disciplined legal reasoning of John Marshall and Joseph Story to the mystical aphorisms of the fortune cookie."

JUSTICE SCALIA: The witness is excused; with our thanks for lunch.

PLAINTIFF's ATTORNEY: I don't understand.

JUSTICE SCALIA: Maybe you will find some wisdom in your fortune cookie, or maybe not. I was in Hong Kong recently for a conference; Chinese restaurants do not have fortune cookies there.

PLAINTIFF's ATTORNEY: I would like to present an expert witness to testify as to the emotional distress and mental anguish that has caused PLAINTIFF's loss of enjoyment of life. I will also call the PLAINTIFF to testify as to her emotional distress and mental suffering.

DEFENDANT's ATTORNEY: First, PLAINTIFF's ATTORNEY has given no notice that he would introduce an expert witness to testify about PLAINTIFF's alleged emotional distress and mental anguish.

(PLAINTIFF, getting ready to go to the witness stand fluffs up her hair and takes out her makeup. She is horrified when she looks in a pocket mirror and sees no reflection; then remembers that she is dead)

DEFENDANT's ATTORNEY: Second, such testimony is not necessary, as PLAINTIFF has not suffered any loss of enjoyment of life as will be established by the exhibits I wish to introduce into evidence. In addition, if you will look at PLAINTIFF's attire you will see the results of her recent shopping spree at the mall the day after she was disqualified for the Mandarin teaching job: new shoes, nice dress, and an expensive Apple watch. We also have some Facebook posts of PLAINTIFF and her friends laughing and eating ice cream in the mall on the same day, and more later on in a bar, drinking Champagne, not the drink of a depressed person.

PLAINTIFF's ATTORNEY: I object to the admission of PLAINTIFF's Facebook posts into evidence.

DEFENDANT's ATTORNEY: Someone told me to save the best for last. Instead of offering the Facebook posts into evidence, I offer the following document.

(DEFENDANT's ATTORNEY approaches the bench and hands a formal looking document to JUSTICE SCALIA and points out that it has been notarized and authenticated)

JUSTICE SCALIA (to PLAINTIFF's ATTORNEY): How much do you know about the PLAINTIFF?

PLAINTIFF's ATTORNEY: She was an English teacher in a small town in New Jersey for several years; then lost her job when the school burnt down and she moved here.

JUSTICE SCALIA: Did you know that her father was a sales representative abroad for an American company?

PLAINTIFF's ATTORNEY (looking worried): Where is this going?

JUSTICE SCALIA: Look at this.

(He hands the document to PLAINTIFF's ATTORNEY and waits)

PLAINTIFF's ATTORNEY: It is a birth certificate.

JUSTICE SCALIA: No Kidding. Read PLAINTIFF's place of birth out loud, for everyone to hear.

PLAINTIFF's ATTORNEY: Shanghai.

DEFENDANT's ATTORNEY: That makes the PLAINTIFF Chinese, so there is no discrimination in favor of Chinese.

JUSTICE SCALIA: Case dismissed, with prejudice.

(With that, he bangs the gavel and there is a crack of thunder, followed by a loud swishing sound. PLAINTIFF finds herself back in Heaven, in front of the Complaint desk)

ST. IVES: Back so soon?

THE END

ALL ABOARD – Last Bus to Canada

(The hallway of the office building is lined on both sides with folding chairs as far as the eye can see; not one seat is empty as the occupants nervously await their turn. A desk has been placed at the end of the hallway, occupied by the bored RECEPTIONIST who is nevertheless busy at work—polishing her nails)

RECEPTIONIST: Next—number 293.

(Number 293 approaches the RECEPTIONIST, hands her a card with the number on it)

RECEPTIONIST: You can go in now, Mr. Smith.

ALAN SMITHEE: My name is Smithee, not Smith.

RECEPTIONIST: Whatever.

(ALAN SMITHEE opens the door and enters a room with a large wooden desk decorated with an overflowing in-box stacked with applications. Behind it sits a friendly well-fed man in his sixties, wearing a dark pinstripe suit, crisp white shirt and solid yellow necktie. He adjusts his cuff links as he motions for ALAN SMITHEE to sit in the chair in front of the desk)

CHIEF OF STAFF: I can only give you ten minutes.

ALAN SMITHEE: I have been waiting for over two hours.

CHIEF OF STAFF: I am sorry about that Mr. Smith, but we have 4,000 positions to fill.

ALAN SMITHEE: It's Smithee, not Smith.

CHIEF OF STAFF: Name sounds familiar—Alan Smithee—can't quite place it. Have we met before?

ALAN SMITHEE: No.

CHIEF OF STAFF: I know I've heard that name before.

ALAN SMITHEE: Many years ago, Hollywood directors who wanted to avoid being named as the director of a film they were unhappy with used a pseudonym, which most often was 'Alan Smithee.'

CHIEF OF STAFF: Oh, so you are a movie director?

ALAN SMITHEE: No.

CHIEF OF STAFF: Then it's your real name?

ALAN SMITHEE: Not at all. I just want to remain anonymous.

CHIEF OF STAFF: Anonymous! How can we hire you if we don't know your name?

ALAN SMITHEE: I am not here about a job. I have a plan to get the President-elect off to a good start.

CHIEF OF STAFF: Why don't you send it to me in writing and I will have someone take a look at it.

(The CHIEF OF STAFF writes an email address on the back of a business card and hands it to ALAN SMITHEE)

ALAN SMITHEE: I can't do that, I want to remain anonymous.

CHIEF OF STAFF: Well, then, I don't think I can help you.

ALAN SMITHEE: It's a question of helping the President-elect, not me. I have a plan to make a goodwill gesture to those who did not vote for the President-elect, unite the country and start rebuilding the infrastructure immediately, all in one step.

CHIEF OF STAFF: It sounds very noble, but I don't have time right now to listen to something that involved.

ALAN SMITHEE: I can explain it very quickly—you said you would give me ten minutes.

(The CHIEF OF STAFF looks at his watch and nods affirmatively)

CHIEF OF STAFF: OK, you have six more minutes.

ALAN SMITHEE: Thank you, you won't be sorry.

CHIEF OF STAFF: Let's hear it.

ALAN SMITHEE: First, California did not vote for the President-elect, so a goodwill gesture would be to start rebuilding the infrastructure in Southern California.

CHIEF OF STAFF: Why there?

ALAN SMITHEE: That's where Hollywood is.

CHIEF OF STAFF: I'm sure that must make sense, but the reasoning escapes me for the moment.

ALAN SMITHEE: That is because the Hollywood community is quite depressed about the election results. Several psychologists and therapists have reported that many of their clients, who are always under extreme pressure anyway, are sinking into depression. That may indirectly cause the population to become depressed and negative.

CHIEF OF STAFF: I don't see the connection.

ALAN SMITHEE: These are the people who produce our motion pictures and TV shows, constantly being watched by millions, especially with streaming these days. What would the mood be if they were suddenly faced with watching only somber, depressing movies and TV shows?

CHIEF OF STAFF: I see your point.

ALAN SMITHEE: Good.

CHIEF OF STAFF: But how is starting to rebuild the infrastructure in Southern California going to help?

ALAN SMITHEE: You start by rebuilding the highways from Los Angeles to Vancouver.

CHIEF OF STAFF: Vancouver?

ALAN SMITHEE: Well, of course you would stop at the border.

CHIEF OF STAFF: Obviously.

ALAN SMITHEE: You might even repair a few bridges along the way, and make detours here and there to avoid any 'Christmas tree' for sale signs when you go through the wooded areas of Oregon and Washington to avoid offending anyone.

CHIEF OF STAFF: You are talking about a project that spans California, Oregon and Washington. How is all of this going to raise the mood in Hollywood?

ALAN SMITHEE: Many of them threatened to move to Canada if their candidate lost.

CHIEF OF STAFF: If they do, they will fly.

ALAN SMITHEE: Not at all. They can be shamed into not flying in their private jets or driving in their gas guzzling Hummers.

CHIEF OF STAFF: Hmm.

ALAN SMITHEE: The government can offer free transportation on Greyhound buses, praising how these passengers are helping the environment by not using their private planes.

CHIEF OF STAFF: Are these people used to riding the bus?

ALAN SMITHEE: Musicians often tour the country on luxury buses; movie stars stay on location in luxury trailers. The Greyhound buses can be spruced up to add some luxury and they will be travelling on new highways.

CHIEF OF STAFF: Even so, it would be a very long ride.

ALAN SMITHEE: I have a solution for that.

(The CHIEF OF STAFF looks skeptical, but remains interested)

CHIEF OF STAFF: I'm listening.

ALAN SMITHEE: Local employment can be increased by building comfortable rest stops along the way, maybe spaced two or three hours apart. They could be decorated with posters from Hollywood films and directors' chairs, with the latest editions of *Variety* and *The Hollywood Reporter* available. Perhaps offer fresh mountain spring water and vegan appetizers free of charge.

CHIEF OF STAFF: I'm not convinced yet. We're still talking about a long ride for a bunch of depressed people in a small space.

ALAN SMITHEE: You haven't heard the best part yet.

CHIEF OF STAFF: Tell me.

ALAN SMITHEE: Each rest stop will have a specially designed room, with soft music, comfortable chairs and a long leather couch.

CHIEF OF STAFF: What's the couch for?

ALAN SMITHEE: Each rest stop will be manned by a psychiatrist or analyst free of charge—more employment.

CHIEF OF STAFF: That's fine, but it will slow down the trip if too many of them need a consultation at a particular stop.

ALAN SMITHEE: I don't think that will be a problem because the rest stops will not be placed that far apart.

CHIEF OF STAFF: Anything else?

ALAN SMITHEE: Yes. Each rest stop will have a drive-through window for those who prefer driving their own car instead of taking the bus.

CHIEF OF STAFF: You seem to have thought of everything.

ALAN SMITHEE: The only problem is if too many of them try to move to Canada.

CHIEF OF STAFF: You mean the cost might escalate.

ALAN SMITHEE: No, Canada might build a wall.

THE END

EU OFFICIALS SUMMONED to MOUNT OLYMPUS

After an all-day session hammering out the latest economic rescue proposal for Greece—actually a take or leave it deal—the meeting adjourns. The underlings leave the room, leaving only those who really matter: the Presidents of the European Council ("TUSK"), the European Commission ("JUNCKER") and the European Central Bank ("DRAGHI"), as well as the President of France ("HOLLAND") and the Chancellor of Germany ("MERKEL"). It is late but many restaurants are still open—though only a few suitable to the standards of the esteemed group. It is ironic that the one they end up at is a Greek restaurant, fortunately one with a Michelin rating—only two stars, but sometimes sacrifices have to be made. The ensemble in elegant dress enters the restaurant where they fit in seamlessly with the other expensively dressed patrons and are ushered into one of the restaurant's elegant private dining rooms.

Appropriate to their status, the meal commences with French champagne, followed by a choice of several house specialties: Roasted figs stuffed with feta cheese; Santorini Fava, with caramelized onions and black truffle vinaigrette, encircled with grilled octopus slices; Greek lamb quince stew; Fried sardines; and finally desert, Yogurt mousse with sour cherry preserves. Later, an after dinner aperitif—a sweet light wine with a unique but pleasant taste—is served by a surly waiter with unruly hair in a uniform that he must have borrowed from someone else. His eyes seem to radiate malice as he quickly refills their glasses. Unknown to them, and in spite of the rules that make it virtually impossible to fire employees of the European Union, he is the only employee known to have been fired by the EU. The effects of the aperitif are quickly realized as the diner's motions slow; their speech slurs as they fall asleep in their chairs. They will eventually awaken, only to find themselves at a distant location.

A short time later the BUS DRIVER looks at his watch, then at the ancient Mercedes bus, one he had never seen or driven before. It was from another era, evidenced by its short stubby length and two-toned finish of blue and white (or was it once crème), or what was left of it. The elements had eaten into the finish, leaving ugly splotches of rust on the sides and top of the vehicle. Still in working order were large round headlights, one on either side of the round Mercedes emblem on the front. The windshield wipers had no doubt once worked, but the BUS DRIVER was not going to test them before he set out. No need to start with a negative omen; it wasn't supposed to rain anyway.

The BUS DRIVER climbs aboard and counts his passengers—one woman with short hair and four gentlemen, or so they might be described if their manner of dress is any guide. The condition of the interior of the bus is no better than the outside, but the passengers do not notice as all are in a deep sleep. The engine sputters, then starts and the bus moves forward. That's when the BUS DRIVER notices that there are no outside mirrors.

The bus drives for several hours, passing through several towns before stopping at Katerini for gas; then it continues onward to Litichoro, the last small village at the foot of Mount Olympus before the journey is interrupted. The old Mercedes bus is travelling at a slow speed, but when it stops suddenly the passengers are thrown forward. Curses in sleepy voices break out in various languages. The bus driver looks through the front window and blows the horn several times without any response. Finally he opens the door, climbs out and approaches an object blocking the road—a wooden bathtub with a man crawled up inside.

DRIVER: What the bloody hell are you doing in the middle of the road?

DIOGENES: Waiting for the bus.

DRIVER: The bus doesn't stop here.

DIOGNES: It just did.

DRIVER: Get that thing out of the way.

DIOGENES: Help me put it on the top of the bus; I'm going with you.

DRIVER: Certainly not.

DIOGENES: Then I am not moving.

(They stare at each other, neither wanting to budge first, until someone in the bus starts blowing the horn)

DRIVER: Oh, very well.

(DIOGENES crawls out of the tub and places a lamp on the ground. They carry the tub to the back of the bus. The DRIVER climbs up the ladder and DIOGENES hoists the tub up to him. The DRIVER pushes the tub onto the roof of the bus and secures it with a rope)

DRIVER (continuing): I hope you are satisfied.

DIOGENES: I will give you a good rating if you have a passenger satisfaction survey to fill out.

DRIVER: Do you realize that we are now behind schedule; there are some very important people on the bus.

DIOGENES: No doubt they think they are.

(DIOGENES gets on the bus and walks to the back, swinging his lamp to get a look at the weary passengers. The DRIVER jumps in and starts the bus; DIOGNENES falls into a seat as the bus lurches forward. The passengers doze off as the bus continues its long journey in the darkness along a narrow road that slowly winds its way up the mountain until it reaches Prionia, where the road ends)

DRIVER: All change please. Mind the gap.

(MERKEL gets off the bus while the others slowly wake up, wondering how they ended up on a bus)

DIOGENES: Are you bozos going to stay here all night?

(The DRIVER hits the horn a few times to wake up the stragglers)

HOLLAND: Who is that rude bum in the back of the bus?

DIOGENES: I am Diogenes, often called *Diogenes the Dog*.

HOLLAND: No wonder. You could use a bath and a haircut.

BUS DRIVER (from the front of the bus): Hey, no comments about haircuts.

DIOGENES (to HOLLAND): I lead a simple life. At least I don't spend 10,000 euros a month on haircuts, not that your stylist has much to work with.

HOLLAND: It's only 9,895 euros.

(One by one the remaining passengers get off the bus and look around, shivering in the cold)

TUSK: Where are we going?

DIOGENES: I thought that you knew everything, especially what is best for others.

TUSK: I wasn't talking to you.

DIOGENES: Were you talking to yourself? If you were, I can recommend a good book on the subject.

(TUSK walks away from DIOGENES)

DRAGHI: What's that awful smell?

DIOGENES: Don't look at me,

(A LARGE MAN in a sheepskin coat and a cigarette dangling from his lips approaches, followed by several donkeys)

JUNCKER: I demand to know what's going on.

LARGE MAN: All aboard. Mount up.

(The group looks around, puzzled and uncertain about what to do)

LARGE MAN: You can either ride or walk, but the mountain gets a bit sleep and sometimes the rocks loosen and fall. You are lucky because the donkeys usually haul supplies, not people.

JUNCKER: I am going nowhere.

LARGE MAN: You're already there—nowhere. If you stay here you will freeze to death by morning.

BUS DRIVER: That would be a big loss, wouldn't it?

(The BUS DRIVER takes off his cap and JUNCKER realizes that he is looking at BORIS JOHNSON)

JUNCKER: It's you.

BORIS JOHNSON: Sorry I can't continue on with you. Maybe we can meet for tea at the Ritz next time you are in London.

(JUNCKER turns away and looks around. Although it is still dark, he realizes that there is nothing for hundreds of kilometers and reluctantly mounts a donkey)

LARGE MAN (to DIOGENES): You going to walk?

DIOGENES: These well-fed bureaucrats must weigh more than the donkeys.

LARGE MAN: Don't concern yourself about the donkeys. They usually carry much heavier loads.

DIOGENES (to MERKEL): I understand that you like hiking. Care to join me?

MERKEL (climbing onto a donkey): Not in these shoes.

(The next day the morning sun is slowly rising above the mist as the passengers begin to awaken in their new surroundings, feeling sore and stiff, wondering where the hell they are)

MERKEL (turning over): Who kicked me?

HOLLAND: It wasn't me.

(They look around and realize that they have been asleep all night in a makeshift barn, together with the donkeys; the one next to MERKEL gets to its feet and moves away. They all fully awaken in response to a loud blast from a trumpet)

DIOGENES: Rise and shine. Today is your big day.

TUSK: What's he talking about?

DIOGENES: Were you speaking to me?

(TUSK turns away from DIOGENES. The trumpet sounds again as a STABLE GROOM enters, dressed like a race track jockey in black cap, red jacket and white pants)

STABLE GROON: Sorry we can't offer you a shower. This will have to do.

(He dusts the straw off their clothes with a whisk broom as they object. HOLLAND adjusts his glasses and brushes his hair back with his hands. MERKEL touches up her hair)

STABLE GROOM: This way, if you please.

(He leads them up to the Pantheon, the highest peak on Mount Olympus, nowadays more commonly known as Mytikas. At the entrance of a courtyard they are welcomed by HERMES, god of travelers and hospitality, as well as thievery and other things. Inside, on a large gold throne at the far end sits ZEUS, surrounded by the other Olympians. The mist makes it appear as though they are suspended on a cloud; perhaps they are. The puzzled travelers walk forward and come to a halt)

HOLLAND: What is this—some kind of Greek theatre?

MERKEL: Maybe a Hollywood movie set.

DRAGHI: No, they are wearing Greek costumes.

DIOGENES: Don't you fools know where you are?

HERMES (to the uninformed): You are on Mount Olympus—in the presence of the twelve Olympians.

(A thunderbolt strikes the ground, and the assembled group jumps)

ZEUS: I see that I now have everyone's attention. FINANCE MINISTER, you may present your case.

JUNCKER: What's the meaning of this?

ZEUS: Silence, mortal.

(ZEUS throws his hand forward and a thunderbolt lands at JUNCKER's feet)

FINANCE MINISTER: The bailout and austerity measures that have been imposed on the Greek people by the EU have caused widespread suffering, economic hardship and social unrest. The billions provided by this so called "rescue plan" have gone 95% to the European Banks.

TUSK (to ZEUS): You have no authority over the European Union.

DRAGHI: I say we leave.

(ZEUS shoots repeated thunderbolts at the feet of JUNCKER, TUSK and DRAGHI. They jump each time and their motion is similar to bullet dancing—shooting close to a victim's feet—in an old western movie.

DIOGENES: I haven't had this much fun in a long time.

(The thunderbolts stop and JUNCKER, TUSK and DRAGHI compose themselves)

DIOGENES: You are all fools, suffering from "endemic tower phobia."

FINANCE MINISTER: That's a new one on me. What does it mean?

DIOGENES: It is a psychological condition that starts each morning during the chauffeur-driven ride by a high-level bureaucrat, most often unelected, to an expensively furnished office in a modern skyscraper that often reaches above the clouds. The condition accelerates faster for those who reach the top floor in a private non-stop elevator in less than sixty seconds. Once seated behind a desk that would have been the envy of the mighty ZEUS …

ZEUS: What's that you say?

(DIOGENES's explanation is interrupted by a loud thunderbolt)

DIOGENES: Begging your pardon, mighty ZEUS. I meant to say King Farouk.

FINANCE MINISTER (to DIOGENES): You were saying …

DIOGENES: Once seated behind a typically gold inlayed desk, the high atmosphere causes the close fitting tailor-made suits of these know-it-all big shots to compress, forcing pressure upwards into their heads, which then swell with self-importance.

FINANCE MINISTER: That explains a lot about dealing with the European Council, the European Commission and the European Central Bank.

JUNCKER: I'm not going to listen to any more of this.

DRAGHI: Nor am I.

TUSK: I didn't come here to be insulted; in fact, I didn't even ask to come here at all.

(ZEUS sends thunderbolts that barely miss the trio's shoes)

ZEUS: One more peep out of you overpaid bureaucrats and the next thunderbolt will make those expensive shoes into open-toed ones.

(Another thunderbolt is shot as a warning)

ZEUS (to FINANCE MINISTER): You may proceed.

MERKEL (to the others): It's not just a bad dream, is it?

THE END

WE ARE BUSY ASSISTING OTHER CUSTOMERS

Please listen carefully as our menu may have changed from the last time you attempted to contact us. We are experiencing unusually high volume and are busy assisting other customers. [Interpretation – The Company is too cheap to hire enough help to answer calls without long wait times.]

If you believe that, please press 1.

Thank you for selecting 1. You will now be added to our telemarketing list, which we sell to others in order to increase net income.

Please stay on the line; we will get to you shortly.

Please press 2 if you need to take a piss while you wait; we will place your call on hold for a minimum of three minutes. If you need more time, please press the number of additional minutes, followed by the pound sign. If you have difficulty pissing, select enough time to avoid being disconnected.

Please press 3 if you need to take a crap while you wait; we will place your call on hold for a minimum of ten minutes; if you need more time, please press the number of additional minutes, followed by the pound sign. We hope everything comes out all right. If not, try eating some prunes before you call us back.

Please press 4 if you need to fart, as our staff members, though low-paid, are sensitive and refined persons not used to hearing crude sounds. Your call will be placed in a special holding pattern until you return to waiting by pressing the pound sign. In the case of multiple farts, we will give you sufficient time to open your window and press the pound sign before disconnecting you.

Please press 5 if you are an impatient person and we will disconnect your call after 60 seconds as we do not wish to add to your anxiety. You might want to consult a doctor about your condition before you call us again. Good luck and Happy Groundhog Day.

Please press 6 if you would like us to call you back one of these days. Hopefully it will be during your lifetime, but if you live in a retirement community who knows?

Please press 7 if you would not like to listen to music while you wait. We have a new song each day, which repeats over and over, and it is likely that you will have the lyrics memorized by the time we get to you.

Thank you for selecting 7. You will now hear one advertisement after another while waiting, and if you wait long enough, you may hear something of interest to you.

Please press 8 if you would like to return merchandise. You should have your address, credit card number and order number ready.

Unfortunately this option is no longer available.

Please press 9 if you would like to return to the main menu.

Thank you for selecting this option. You will now be disconnected. Have a nice day.

NOTE: If you call back later the line might still be busy.

THE END

FRENCH INCIVILITY BRIGADE v. DOG POOP STREET ART

The hearings of the Committee on Legal Affairs, on recommendation of the Working Group on Copyright, take place in one of the EU's modern cost-is-no-object buildings, with ceilings in the lobby so high that Michelangelo could never have painted murals on it unless he wore an oxygen mask and learned to levitate. The hearings today are being held in one of the smaller rooms of the cost-is-no-object building as not all members of the Committee on Legal Affairs are scheduled to be present.

Two members in long black robes with white wing collars are seated on a dais, three steps—not merely one or two steps—above the floor in the small but well-appointed meeting room. Their shoes, no doubt expensive, are hidden from view by a long mahogany piece of furniture, similar to a long bench or credenza, which curves at an angle of 10 mm per 10 cm of length—the same as the maximum EU curvature rules allowed for Class I cucumbers. The EU flag flies from a pole at either end of the dais.

Their serious faces cast an impression that they have been frozen in time, possibly waiting for Doctor Who to appear. Actually, they are waiting for the third member—the Chairman—to arrive before they begin. In front of the dais are several rows of chairs, divided by a wide aisle in the middle. An usher walks up and down the aisle, quietly offering peanuts or popcorn for three Euros or beer for 6 Euros. The Committee members are not happy about this, but it was one of the conditions of the vendor for selling his shop and small piece of land to the EU.

A Page enters, dressed similar to the Swiss Guards at the Vatican, and blows a trumpet.

PAGE: All rise.

(Everyone stands as the CHAIRMAN enters. The PAGE walks to a small stand, pushes a button and the national anthem of the EU starts rolling. The CHAIRMAN puts both hands to his head in agony)

CHAIRMAN: Turn that thing off. I have an awful hangover … I mean headache. No offence to Schiller or Beethoven, but I do not need "Ode to Joy" this morning, not after last night.

(The music stops. The CHAIRMAN takes his place the center of the dais and the PAGE tells those in the audience to be seated)

VICE-CHAIRMAN: It looks more like a hangover.

CHAIRMAN: Last night I violated one of most important principles of civilization.

VICE-CHAIRMAN: Which one?

CHAIRMAN: Never drink cheap wine.

VICE-CHAIRMAN: You drank cheap wine? I am appalled.

CHAIRMAN: It was not my fault. We had guests over last night and one of them brought a cheap bottle of wine, the name of which I would never utter in your presence.

VICE-CHAIRMAN: I certainly hope not, but why did you drink it?

CHAIRMAN: My wife opened the bottle, filled the glasses and passed them around before I could say anything. I had no choice.

VICE-CHAIRMAN: There is always a choice.

CHAIRMAN: Not when your brother-in-law brings the wine. Unfortunately, he is above even the slightest criticism in our house; I have to pretend to be nice to him when he visits.

VICE-CHAIRMAN: That must be difficult.

CHAIRMAN: Not really; I took acting lessons some time ago.

(The PAGE departs and is replaced by the CLERK, dressed in a dark suit, much like a funeral director)

CHAIRMAN (to the CLERK): What is the first item on today's agenda?

CLERK: There is a conflict between the recently introduced French Incivility Brigade and the rights of street artists, one in particular. That is all I know, being a lowly civil servant and not privy to the documents filed in this matter.

CHAIRMAN: Well, I have not seen them either. Are representatives here to represent all of the stakeholders who have an interest in this matter?

CLERK: Yes—the injured party and representatives of the French Incivility Brigade, Paris street artists, the French Patrolmen's Association, and Professor Mockingbird, a copyright expert and author of *Soft Sculpture and Copyright*.

CHAIRMAN: Call the first witness.

CLERK: First witness, representing the French Incivility Brigade.

CHAIRMAN (to BRIGADE WITNESS): Can you explain what the French Incivility Brigade is?

BRIGADE WITNESS: Yes, Excellency.

CHAIRMAN: That sounds nice, but Chairman will do.

BRIGADE WITNESS: A little history, if I may?

CHAIRMAN: Be brief.

BRIGADE WITNESS: Of course. Several years ago Paris had a fleet of Motocrottes, but …

VICE-CHAIRMAN (interrupting): What is a Motocrotte?

BRIGADE WITNESS: A motorized pooper-scooper, used to pick up dog poop. They were expensive and later abandoned after it was determined that they were only collecting about 20% of the dog shit on the streets of Paris.

COMMITTEE AVOCAT: I skipped breakfast in order to get here on time to hear about dog shit in Paris?

BRIGADE WITNESS: There are more important issues involved.

COMMITTEE AVOCAT: I certainly hope so.

BRIGADE WITNESS: Paris has recently established an Incivility Brigade of about 2,000 security agents to hand out warnings and fines to those who commit antisocial behavior. They will be uniformed and armed with teargas spray and wooden-handled truncheons.

COMMITTEE AVOCAT: I assume that they are going to deal with bank robbers, jewelry store heists and other serious crimes.

BRIGADE WITNESS: Not exactly. They are going to track down and punish men who urinate against walls in public, litter-bugs who toss cigarette butts on the street and dog owners who do not clean up after their dogs poop on the sidewalk.

VICE-CHAIRMAN: I do not understand how this involves the EU.

BRIGADE WITNESS: The legality of the Incivility Brigade has been challenged by certain street art groups and artists in Paris. Artists in other parts of Europe are likely to encounter similar problems.

VICE-CHAIRMAN: That is an odd one; I would have thought that the dog owners in Paris would be the ones against it.

BRIGADE WITNESS: There have been some demonstrations but no legal action ... well, only one.

CHAIRMAN: Please explain, but be brief.

BRIGADE WITNESS: The Mayor was finishing lunch at his favorite outdoor café and an angry dog owner approached him and complained about the new Incivility

Brigade. One of the Mayor's aides stood and told the dog owner to leave or he would be arrested; then stamped his foot to scare off the dog, sat and asked for the bill. Unnoticed by the Mayor or his aide, the dog made a deposit under the Mayor's chair before running off. After the bill was paid, the Mayor slipped in a pile of dog shit when he got up to leave. A nearby policeman was called to chase after the dog owner and arrest him.

CHAIRMAN: We need to move along. Who is next?

CLERK: The representative of the French Patrolmen's Association.

CHAIRMAN (to ASSOCIATION WITNESS): Are you here in support of the Incivility Brigade?

ASSOCIATION WITNESS: Not at all. We are against them.

CHAIRMAN: Please explain.

ASSOCIATION WITNESS: We are all in favor of cleaning up crime in Paris, even cigarette butts.

CHAIRMAN: Not dog shit?

ASSOCIATION WITNESS: No. First, Parisians love their dogs and are extremely unhappy with the Incivility Brigade; they will express their anger at all law enforcement officers, including us. Second, it is easier to catch criminals engaged in street crime when they slip on dog shit. We have special non-skid boots, so it is not a problem for us.

CHAIRMAN: Thank you for your insight; you are excused. Is there someone here to represent the street artists?

STREET ARTIST WITNESS (standing): Right here.

CHAIRMAN: What do street artists have against the activities of the French Incivility Brigade?

STREET ARTIST WITNESS: Their enforcement actions will in some cases violate the protections of street artists under copyright laws.

CHAIRMAN: Such as?

STREET ARTIST WITNESS: The right to integrity—not to have your work altered, or the right to reproduce and sell your work—which disappears if your work is removed or destroyed by overzealous officers.

COMMITTEE AVOCAT: Have there been any cases of street art being removed or destroyed?

STREET ARTIST WITNESS: Yes. We brought a victim— the person who filed the initial complaint.

CHAIRMAN: Very well, next witness.

(The next witness is a dog owner, but not the one arrested by the Mayor)

DOG OWNER: I live in Paris in the 20th Arrondissement, where street art is encouraged, at least if it is on a wall.

COMMITTEE AVOCAT: Where is yours?

DOG OWNER: On the ground.

COMMITTEE AVOCAT: Be more specific—the sidewalk, the pavement?

DOG OWNER: On the sidewalk, but either would qualify for copyright protection. An idea or artistic expression, such as street art, requires little if any creativity, but it must be fixed in some tangible form to be protected under copyright laws.

VICE-CHAIRMAN: We all know the basic principles of copyright law. Why are you here?

DOG OWNER: Because the EU has been revising its rules to provide harmonization of copyright law throughout the 28 member nations. Criminal and copyright laws are in conflict in France; now it the time to sort this out and provide uniformity throughout the EU.

CHAIRMAN: Proceed, if you must.

DOG OWNER: The French Incivility Brigade destroyed one of my sculptures and gave me three fines.

CHAIRMAN: You are talking about street art, correct?

DOG OWNER: Yes. The first fine was for my dog pissing on a fire hydrant. I did not challenge that because the dog piss just went down into the gutter instead of creating anything in a fixed form. Next, my dog started walking away and the officer yelled at him. The poor thing was so scared that he made an extra big poop on the sidewalk. I lit a cigarette to calm down, looked at the poop and could not believe what I saw. It looked very much like a face, with an uncanny resemblance to the officer. I started laughing and stubbed out my cigarette. Then I stuck the butt in the dog shit just where the mouth should be.

COMMITTEE AVOCAT: I bet that went over well with the officer.

DOG OWNER: He gave me a fine for dog litter and another for the cigarette butt. When I refused to clean it up he shoved me with his truncheon and I stumbled onto the dog shit, destroying my street art.

VICE-CHAIRMAN: I believe that there is a case pending in the United States Court of Appeals for the 9th Circuit—Naruto v. Slater—which involves the question of whether or not an animal may be a copyright owner. If we adopted such a rule in the EU, your dog would own the copyright, not you, in the event that this particular dog poop constituted an artistic expression in fixed form. On the other hand, you might be the author of the dog poop face if you directed your dog where and when to shit, also taking into account your placement of the cigarette butt.

COMMITTEE AVOCAT: Let me interject. Depending on the consistency of the dog poop, it may be in fixed form only temporarily; and thus not entitled to copyright protection by anyone.

DOG OWNER: I would like Professor Mockingbird to testify on that point.

COMMITTEE AVOCAT: Professor, do you have a first name?

PROFESSOR MOCKINGBIRD: Yes, but I prefer not to say it.

COMMITTEE AVOCAT: I am afraid we need it for the record if you are going to testify.

PROFESSOR MOCKINGBIRD (in a soft voice): Elmo.

COMMITTEE AVOCAT: Professor, could you please speak up?

PROFESSOR MOCKINGBIRD (louder): Elmo.

(Everyone in the committee room starts laughing, until silenced by the CHAIRMAN)

COMMITTEE AVOCAT: I am sorry to hear that, but what are your qualifications?

PROFESSOR MOCKINGBIRD: I am the author of *Soft Sculpture and Copyright*, available in either French or English. If you would care to buy a copy, it is available online from Amazon and other booksellers. I am also a guest lecturer on the topic of street art at many universities throughout Europe.

COMMITTEE AVOCAT: My understanding is that for purposes of copyright law, a work is considered to be fixed when it is embodied in a tangible, stable and concrete form. Works that are transitory in nature are not protectable under copyright law as they are not fixed. Would you not agree with that, Professor?

PROFESSOR MOCKINGBIRD: Yes, as to dog piss, but not as to street art in the form of soft sculpture.

COMMITTEE AVOCAT: Would you care to define soft sculpture.

PROFESSOR MOCKINGBIRD: Street art is typically painted on a wall, on the side of a building or sometimes on the pavement. Soft sculpture is often attached to something, such as a building or a park bench, but can be placed on the ground or pavement. Although soft sculpture typically is made from rubber, latex or cloth, there is no reason why soft sculpture cannot consist of dog shit.

COMMITTEE AVOCAT: How can dog poop on the sidewalk be deemed to be in fixed form? It is transitory, ready to be swept away or washed away in the rain.

PROFESSOR MOCKINGBIRD: That is not necessarily so, especially in the non-rainy season. Once in fixed form, copyright attaches, even though the creation may subsequently be destroyed. For example, suppose I write a lecture on a piece of paper, read it to an audience and then destroy the paper; my copyright continues.

VICE-CHAIRMAN: Professor, are you sure that you want your lecture notes to be compared with a pile of dog shit?

PROFESSOR MOCKINGBIRD: Never mind.

CHAIRMAN: The EU has received more than enough criticism over the volume of its directives and regulations. We do not need to add dog shit to the list. Hearing adjourned.

CLERK: All rise. Watch your step when you leave the building.

THE END

PERSONA – the New Miracle Drug

Who needs *big pharma* anyway? A hitherto unknown pharmaceutical company incorporated in one of the lesser-known tax haven islands in the Coral Sea (east of Australia) today filed an application with the United States Food and Drug Administration (FDA) for approval of its new drug PERSONA. Extracts from the filing are as follows.

BENEFITS: Relief for persons with irritable personalities. Does everyone think that you are a jerk—even your own mother? Our new miracle drug will make you as lovable as a cute panda.

INGREDIENTS: Panda urine extracted from the bark of pine trees where pandas have relieved themselves, combined with three common herbs frequently found in your kitchen.

AUTHOR's COMMENT: Although naming the herbs is not likely to allow you to replicate PERSONA, disclosure might give the impression that the new miracle drug was excessively priced.

SIDE EFFECTS (also sometimes called severe adverse reactions):

Bladder pain

Blindness (usually temporary)

Bloating

Blurred vision (no worse than after a few too many drinks)

Constipation (you have probably had this before anyway)

Dizziness

Frequent craving to eat bamboo shoots (avoid using chopsticks in Chinese restaurants)

Itching (could be anywhere or everywhere)

Loss of balance (more common with left-handed persons)

Nausea (stay close to the toilet)

Numbness (usually in the feet and nose)

Rash (sometimes resembling a Spotted Sandpiper or similar bird, but the spots are red)

Risk of falling and bone fractures (try to land on your ass, not your hands)

Shortness of breath

Vomiting (carry a large plastic bag while taking PERSONA)

AUTHOR's COMMENT: If you carry a plastic bag while walking your dog, don't forget to bring an extra bag for yourself.

OTHER SIDE EFFECTS:

Farting during sex

THE END

WONDERFUL AIRWAYS – Check-in Counter

(The scene is a Wonderful Airways [WA] terminal on a Bank Holiday weekend during which WA has suffered another disruption of its IT system—this time a complete meltdown of its worldwide system. Lines snake back and forth in the departure hall and outside as far as the eye can see. A disgruntled male passenger finally reaches the front of the line and confronts the female agent behind the counter at one of the few check-in positions that is open. He is dressed casually, wearing a short-sleeved shirt that reveals a large bruise on his left arm and a broken wristwatch)

WA AGENT: May I help you?

PASSENGER: I doubt it?

WA AGENT: We are doing the best we can, Sir.

PASSENGER: Do you know how long I have been waiting in line?

WA AGENT: I have no idea, but if you like I can make a guess.

PASSENGER: Never mind.

(The PASSENGER looks at the broken watch on his left wrist and places his hand on the counter with a thump)

PASSENGER (continuing): What time is it? As you can see my watch is broken and my arm is bruised.

WA AGENT: Sorry about that.

PASSENGER: Would you like to hear how it happened?

WA AGENT: Not really, Sir. Right now we are very busy.

PASSENGER: I will tell you anyway, since it is WA's fault.

(The WA AGENT drums her fingers on the counter impatiently)

PASSENGER: After queueing for several hours I finally made it inside the terminal and eventually found a place to lie down alongside several other passengers in close quarters where we were furnished with yoga mats. I must have dozed off for a bit, but woke up suddenly with severe pain in my arm. One of the passengers was trying to step over me, but ended up stepping on my arm and breaking my watch.

WA AGENT: That's most unfortunate, but all passengers are suffering some kind of inconvenience because of the delays.

PASSENGER: I expect the airline to reimburse me.

WA AGENT: You will have to file your claim for compensation online.

PASSENGER: How can I do that when your IT system is dead?

WA AGENT: I really don't know, Sir. It's not my department. You might phone customer service for information. They may be able to help.

PASSENGER: When pigs fly.

WA AGENT: Excuse me?

PASSENGER: As I said, we were furnished with yoga mats but after a while I started getting a stiff neck. When I asked one of your staff about pillows, he said it would cost £7.

WA AGENT: That's not right, Sir.

PASSENGER: Probably wanted to take advantage of the situation and make a little money on the side.

WA AGENT: Not at all, Sir. Our new CEO raised the price to £12 for pillows.

PASSENGER: You got to be kidding.

WA AGENT: No, Sir. We at WA take our pricing very seriously.

PASSENGER: Pretty soon you will probably cut out all amenities on board.

WA AGENT: I doubt that. Management seems to adding charges for every item we provide, no matter how small. Prices are listed for all amenities, as you can see from the notice behind me.

(The PASSENGER looks up and reads the notice out loud)

PASSENGER: Peanuts, 5p each; paper napkin, 10p; recycled water, £1.50; plastic cup to hold the water, 75p; key to unlock and lower tray table, £1; toilet paper, £3; use of toilet (3 minute limit), £5.

WA AGENT: You will need to have exact change as no change will be given on board. If you wish to pay by debit or credit card there will be an additional convenience fee of £2.

PASSENGER: You will probably start charging for a cushion on the seats inside the plane next.

WA AGENT: What an excellent idea. If I submit that as an employee suggestion I may get an award.

(The WA AGENT looks at the line behind the PASSENGER)

WA AGENT (continuing): Is there anything else I can help you with?

PASSENGER: Yes, I need a new boarding pass since my flight was changed.

WA AGENT: I'm sorry but the printer is not working.

PASSENGER: Maybe you can just write one out by hand.

WA AGENT: Even if I could do that, I don't have any paper.

PASSENGER: Use this. Be careful; it's the only one I have.

(The PASSENGER places a paper napkin of the counter. The WA AGENT looks at the napkin; then at her watch)

WA AGENT: Oh, look what time it is. My shift is over. Good luck and thank you for choosing WA.

(The WA AGENT walks off and is soon replaced with a new agent)

PASSENGER: I would like …

NEW AGENT: Sorry, but my shift doesn't start for five more minutes.

(The NEW AGENT takes a bottle of nail polish from her purse and places it on the counter)

NEW AGENT (continuing): I know you have been waiting for quite some time, so a few more minutes should not matter.

ANNOUNCEMENT (over loudspeaker): We at Wonderful Airways are truly sorry for the delays that you have experienced and are doing everything possible to remedy the situation and get you to your destinations. You will hear a personal message from our CEO just as soon as he has finished his afternoon tea.

PASSENGER: Cobblers.

NEW AGENT: What did you say?

(The NEW AGENT starts polishing her nails, spills a few drops of polish on the counter and picks up the napkin to wipe it up)

PASSENGER: I mean to say bollocks.

(The PASSENGER slams his right fist of the counter and the bottle of nail polish spills all over)

NEW AGENT: Well, really. There is no need to get upset over a delay; it happens all the time.

THE END

97

PIG SHIT and MOONSHINE – an Alternative Fuel?

SCENE: United States Department of Energy, Washington, D.C., office of Rick Perry, Energy Secretary.

(The telephone rings and PERRY answers)

CALLER: Rick Perry?

PERRY: Yeah.

CALLER: This is Al.

PERRY: Al who?

CALLER: Al Gore.

PERRY: I've heard the name somewhere.

GORE: Former Vice President of the United States, Nobel Peace Prize winner, as well as a Grammy Award and an Academy Award.

PERRY: I was just kidding.

GORE: I recently saw your interview online with the Prime Minister of the Ukraine.

PERRY: Rather embarrassing.

GORE: The most interesting part was allegedly making fuel with a mix of home-brewed alcohol and pig manure based on an invention by the Ukrainian President.

PERRY: You don't have to remind me. I wish people would forget about it.

GORE: Well, you're lucky there's one person who did not forget.

PERRY: Who is that?

GORE: A pig farmer in Tennessee.

PERRY: Are you sure you are Al Gore?

GORE: Absolutely. Ask me anything about climate change and global warming.

PERRY (to himself): Oh God, if I let him start on global warming I'll be on the phone for hours.

(PERRY looks at his watch)

PERRY (to GORE): That's OK. I believe you. You said something about a pig farmer.

GORE: Yes. He has a son at MIT.

PERRY: Good for him.

GORE: That's the Massachusetts Institute of Technology.

PERRY: I know that.

GORE: You'll never guess what his major is.

PERRY: Probably not.

GORE: Chemistry.

PERRY: That's a great story - Son of an American pig farmer gets a degree in chemistry at MIT.

GORE: That's not the story.

PERRY: What is it, then?

GORE: The son came home for summer vacation and of course had to help out on the pig farm. The rest of the time he was on the internet or his smart phone. He saw your interview with the Prime Minister of the Ukraine and showed it to his father.

PERRY: You mean the interview with the fake Prime Minister of the Ukraine.

GORE: Of course, but the farmer asked his son if it was possible to make fuel out of moonshine and pig shit.

PERRY: Obviously not.

GORE: Wrong.

PERRY: Wrong?

GORE: The farmer has a cabin in the mountains in Tennessee and outside is an old-fashioned still where he makes moonshine.

PERRY: Is that legal?

GORE: Only if you have the right licenses.

PERRY: I take it that he doesn't.

GORE: We'll skip over that for now.

PERRY: Where is this going?

GORE: It's going to help the environment and make somebody rich.

PERRY: You mean the pig farmer?

GORE: No, his son the inventor.

PERRY: Don't tell me that he can produce fuel by mixing moonshine with pig shit.

GORE: He's already done it.

PERRY: Then I guess anybody can do it.

GORE: Not at all. He tested mixing different kinds of moonshine from all over Tennessee with pig shit from his father's farm, but nothing worked except when he used the moonshine from his father's still. The local water has something to do with it.

PERRY: How much has he produced?

GORE: Not that much. He needs a grant of about $250,000 to produce more fuel and do proper testing, enlarge the still and get the proper licenses.

PERRY: You mean a grant from the Department of Energy.

GORE: That's why I'm calling.

PERRY: Thanks to the President, our research grant programs have been suspended and may be terminated.

GORE: All of them?

PERRY: I'm not sure.

GORE: Just think; if this is a success it will make monkeys out of all those people who laughed at you because of the fake telephone interview.

PERRY: That would be nice, very nice.

GORE: $250,000 is not that much when you think about the overall benefits to the world.

PERRY: That's true. Maybe I could squeeze the money from somewhere in the budget, but I need to see some evidence that this is a viable project and inspect the still and understand the process.

GORE: The still has to be expanded but you can see it in operation, and meet the farmer and his son.

PERRY: What are the names of the farmer and his son?

GORE: Not over the phone, with the number of leaks in Washington these days.

PERRY: Of course not. What was I thinking?

GORE: I don't want to mention the name of the area or the airport so I will have tickets delivered to your office, for your signature only. Will Saturday work?

PERRY: Absolutely.

(On Saturday morning PERRY takes an early flight on a propeller airplane to a small town in Tennessee, where he is met by the FARMER in a pickup truck. They drive for a half hour or so until they arrive at the farm, located at the end of a dirt road in a wooded area with rolling hills)

PERRY: Where's GORE?

FARMER: He's inside.

(Once inside PERRY meets the FARMER's son, the CHEMIST, and they find GORE in the kitchen)

GORE: Glad you could make it. I see you have already met the CHEMIST.

PERRY: You look a bit different from the last time I saw your photos. Your beard and mustache are a little longer but it looks like you lost some weight.

GORE: Yes, but not easy.

FARMER: Shall we take a look around the farm? You might want to take off your shoes first and wear some boots.

(Now wearing boots, they tour the farm, see pigs foraging in the woods, and learn how pig shit is collected)

CHEMIST: I guess you would like to view the still now?

PERRY: Yes, I want to take a close look.

(They hike through the woods, with the trees getting closer together, until they come to a run-down looking log cabin. The still is outside, behind the log cabin, and the CHEMIST demonstrates how it works; then they go inside the log cabin)

PERRY (to CHEMIST): I want to understand how this conversion process works before I can commit any government funding.

CHEMIST (to PERRY): Taste this.

(The CHEMIST hands PERRY a Mason jar of moonshine. PERRY tastes it and reacts)

PERRY: Quite strong.

CHEMIST (to PERRY): Take a whiff of this.

(The CHEMIST holds a small container of pig shit up to PERRY's nose, and PERRY jumps back. The CHEMIST mixes some moonshine with pig shit and places it into a strange looking machine, which begins to turn inside and emit strange noises)

FARMER: This takes a while. Why don't you city folks sit down and we'll have something to eat.

(They sit on benches at a wooden table as the FARMER prepares and serves breakfast—eggs over easy, grits with gravy, hash-browns and Spam. The CHEMIST offers GORE and PERRY a glass of moonshine, but PERRY politely refuses)

PERRY: Thanks, but I've got to keep a clear head to verify this process. Black coffee would be good, though.

(They take their time eating and finish just as the machine makes a loud noise and shuts off. The CHEMIST then extracts a strange looking liquid—the fuel—and places it into a small air compressor to demonstrate that the fuel works)

CHEMIST: Satisfied?

PERRY: Seems like it works, but obviously it needs to be tested on a much larger scale.

CHEMIST: We'll start immediately when we get the Department of Energy's grant.

(The CHEMIST gives PERRY instructions on where to send the funds, c/o the FARMER, addressed to general delivery at the nearest post office. Later, the CHEMIST drives GORE and PERRY to the airport in the FARMER's truck. GORE says he has a later flight to a different destination and they say goodbye to Perry. GORE and the CHEMIST watch as PERRY goes through the security checkpoint for his flight to Washington)

GORE: That went rather well.

CHEMIST: Yes. You did a fine job impersonating Al Gore.

GORE: Well, I have been acting for many years and I do bear a resemblance to Al Gore.

CHEMIST: Please thank the casting agency.

GORE: Are you really majoring in chemistry major at MIT?

CHEMIST: Chemistry was my high school major. Now I am working as a magician.

GORE: You certainly did a fine job with the demonstration.

CHEMIST: We'll split the money three ways when it arrives.

(After a shaky ride on a prop airplane to Washington, PERRY walks through the terminal toward the exit. Everyone seems to be in a hurry and a tall clean-shaven man bumps into him)

PERRY: You look kind of like Al Gore, without the beard and mustache.

GENTLEMAN: I am Al Gore.

PERRY: Are you sure?

GENTLEMAN: Absolutely.

PERRY (slapping his forehead): Oh shit.

GENTLEMAN: Excuse me?

<u>THE END</u>

BEWARE the REVERSE MORTGAGE

The elderly couple lived on a tree-lined street close to the downtown area of a small town that had seen better times, much better. Unemployment had contributed to the decline, but did not directly affect the retired couple. Then that controversial word *gentrification* reared its ugly head. As often happens, gentrification starts off slowly and suddenly accelerates. Neighboring houses were torn down and replaced by much larger, more expensive homes. The spread between the fixed income of the retired couple and the cost of living kept increasing, primarily because of big property tax increases on their home due to its location. Many others affected by this situation had moved out, but not them. It would never happen, not after fifty plus years in this cozy home. Still, something had to be done.

Walter and Grace were watching one of their favorite TV programs, actually Grace's favorite, when it was interrupted by the advertisement about reverse mortgages for the third time. They had been thinking about it for some time. It all seemed so simple. That nice looking actor on the TV told them that he used to think there might be a catch to reverse mortgages, but not so he assured them repeatedly. You could use the money for whatever you wanted—payment of medical bills, home improvements, new car, maybe a boat or a vacation in Las Vegas or Italy. The best thing was that you didn't have to pay the loan back. Just spend the money.

Grace turned down the volume on the TV, picked up her cell phone and started punching in the numbers on the TV screen.

"What are you doing?" Walter asked.

"Calling the 800 number," Grace said. "It's time we did something."

"Let me have the phone," Walter said, as he reached for it.

Grace handed the phone to him and said, "I thought you were never going to call."

"I will," said Walter, cutting off the call, "but not them. I don't like their advertising; it irritates me."

"I think you are jealous of that good looking actor," Grace said.

"Actors don't know anything about business," Walter said. "They are paid to say that the sponsor has a wonderful product—probably most of them never use the product they are advertising."

"He doesn't look old enough to need a reverse mortgage," Grace said.

"Don't let the heavy makeup fool you," Walter said. "This guy has been around too long to actually be as young as he looks on TV, but I doubt that he has ever gotten a reverse mortgage."

"I thought we agreed to get a reverse mortgage, or at least look into it," Grace said.

"Absolutely," Walter said. "I'm going to look on the internet for companies that offer reverse mortgages and do a comparison."

"When," Grace asked.

"Right now," said Walter, who went over to a small desk and turned on his computer and began a search. Finally satisfied, Walter made an appointment with a mortgage broker for the next day and gave him driving instructions to the house.

***

The following morning Mr. Huff drove up to the residence that was seeking a reverse mortgage, parked in the driveway and rang the doorbell at exactly 11 a.m. Walter opened the door and said, "Right on time."

Walter looked outside toward the driveway at a used Chevrolet with a dented front left fender. Mr. Huff quickly said, "That's a loaner; the only one they had available. I had to leave my Jaguar at the dealer for maintenance again. Jaguars are wonderful cars, but they do require a bit of maintenance. You know how it is."

Walter didn't know how it is, or how it was. He invited Mr. Huff inside and introduced him to Grace.

"Have a seat on the rocker, Mr. Huff," said Grace. "It's really quite relaxing." Across the room, directly opposite the rocker, the TV was on with the volume turned down.

"Actually, it's Captain Huff, but you can call me Charlie," he responded.

"What branch of the services were you in?" Walter asked.

"Special Services," said Huff, immediately regretting his choice as that was merely the entertainment branch of the military. Actually his only service as a Captain had been with the Salvation Army a few years ago.

"I suppose you can't talk about it or you'd have to kill us," Walter said with a serious look, before his face relaxed into a grin.

"Let's get down to business," said Grace.

"Of course," said Huff. He opened his briefcase and handed them each a glossy folder with photos and charts, then explained the reverse mortgage program as they reviewed the materials.

The TV had switched to a commercial—about reverse mortgages. "Oh, look," said Grace, pointing to the TV.

Huff jumped up to turn off the TV, but instead by mistake turned the volume up for all to hear "until the last one leaves the home," then turned it off and returned to the rocking chair.

"That's standard for all reverse mortgages," Huff said. "I suppose you both know what that means?"

"When I kick the bucket," said Walter.

Walter's comment was correct as far as it went, but Huff was here to sell a reverse mortgage; why complicate things?

"I'd rather not think about it," said Grace.

"Never mind that," Walter said. "How much can we get?"

"Let me run some numbers," Huff said. He pulled out a notepad and calculator and asked, "Are there any loans against the property?"

"About $40,000.00," said Walter.

"That will have to be paid off out of the reverse mortgage proceeds," said Huff.

Walter and Grace looked at each other. "Wait," said Grace. "I have an idea. Why can't we just leave the existing mortgage in place and continue making the payments ourselves?"

"That's a good one," said Huff.

"Thank you," said Grace, not really understanding Huff's meaning.

"That's not the way it works," said Huff. "The new lender wants title to the property to be clear of any liens or other mortgage loans."

"I suppose that you are going to deduct other expenses," said Walter.

"Only a few," said Huff.

"Could you be more specific," said Walter.

Huff hesitated before he said, "Costs would include a title search, appraisal fees, recording fees, taxes, postage, termite inspection, preparation of legal documents, etc., etc.."

"And your commission," said Grace.

"Well, yes," said Huff. "I do have to do quite a bit of work, seeking a loan with the best rates for your reverse mortgage, seeing that all of the paperwork gets done on time, etc., etc.."

"After all of those etceteras, how much will we get?" Walter asked.

Huff made a few notations on his notepad and used the calculator to come up with the net amount—$63,200.00.

Walter and Grace looked at each other and agreed that it would have to do. Walter said, "We were hoping to take a vacation in a few weeks if we can get this reverse mortgage done in time."

"No problem," said Huff. "We can start right now. I have the preliminary paperwork here, but there will be a few more documents to sign after the loan is approved." He took out an eleven page contract, filled in several blanks and handed it to Walter. "You both should read it over before you sign."

"You read it, Walter. I get vertigo every time I try to read small print," said Grace.

Walter started to read, and then stopped. "I need to find a magnifying glass," he said. He looked in the desk unsuccessfully, went into the kitchen and returned with an opened box of Crackerjack in his hand. He poured some into his hand, offered it to Huff, who declined, and popped it into his own mouth.

"What are you doing, Walter?" Grace asked.

"I am looking for a magnifying glass." Walter shook out another handful of Crackerjack, retrieved something with his other hand and held up a tiny magnifying glass for the others to see, then ate the handful of Crackerjack. "I usually throw away the toys in boxes but I saved this one."

Walter sat and resumed reading the eleven page document, pausing occasionally to use the tiny magnifying glass, and then started skimming over the remaining pages rapidly.

"Did you read over the whole document carefully?" Huff asked Walter.

"Yes," said Walter. "I'm a speed reader," a phrase Walter had heard somewhere, though it did not accurately describe his reading habits.

"Any questions, either of you?" said Huff. "If not let's get this document signed."

***

When the reverse mortgage loan was approved all that was needed was to wire the money to the borrowers' account and get a receipt signed. Huff had not slept well the night before, woke up with a headache and realized that he was going to be late for his appointment. He jumped in his car, the so-called loaner, and stopped at a Starbucks drive-through window on the way. They had bananas at the window so Huff decided to add a banana to his small black coffee. He finished his coffee by the time he drove up to the driveway, peeled back the banana and started eating it as he walked toward the front door. Huff looked rather silly—briefcase in one hand and banana peel in the other—so he tossed the banana peel over his shoulder.

Once inside, Huff took a computer from his briefcase, got online and transferred the funds to the borrowers' bank account. They signed a receipt, thanked Huff and he left.

Walter put the receipt in his desk and they sat at the kitchen table for a late breakfast.

"Where's my morning paper?" Walter asked.

"I though you got it earlier," said Grace. "It must still be outside. Do you want me to get it?"

"No, I'll go." Walter walked to the front door, opened it and saw the newspaper lying in the driveway. What he did not see was the banana peel that Huff had tossed over his shoulder. Walter slipped and fell, hitting his head against a solid ceramic pot that housed a geranium bush. If he were not unconscious, Walter would have said that he had always hated geraniums, as well as a few choice words.

***

Even during bad times Walter always said that they could get better or they could get worse. This time they only got worse. First was the hospital, where Walter stayed for several weeks. Grace decided to rent a room across from the hospital so that she could be near Walter, and during the last week of her absence decided to have the house painted as a surprise for Walter when he came home. However, Walter's condition deteriorated so much that he had to move into a nursing home—directly from the hospital. Fortunately there was enough money left over from the reverse mortgage financing to make the large deposit that the nursing home required. After Walter was settled in, Grace went to their freshly painted home. She fixed herself a drink, a good stiff one, and sat in the rocking chair. She had another one and sat rocking until she fell asleep. Sometime later she awoke to the sound of a loud noise outside the front door.

She opened the door and saw a workman pounding a wooden sign into the ground. "What are you doing?" she yelled as she went round to read the sign, which said FOR SALE. The workman finished planting the sign and looked at his watch just as a tired looking blue Chevrolet drove up. Out stepped Huff, who thanked the workman and handed him a twenty dollar bill.

Grace approached Huff as another car drove up—a Mercedes—and parked next to the Chevrolet.

Grace started yelling at Huff saying repeatedly, "What's going on." The chunky man from the Mercedes joined them and was introduced as Mr. Slick, the lawyer for the mortgage company, who would explain everything if Grace would just calm down.

They went into the living room and Huff gave Grace another glass of whiskey. Slick handed Grace the loan document and asked if the signature was hers. Of course it was. Next, Slick asked Grace if she had read the document before signing it.

"No", Grace said. "Walter read it."

"Just above the signature lines it says that you and your husband acknowledge that you have read it," said Slick.

"I don't understand what's going on," said Grace. "Why is there a FOR SALE sign in front of my house?"

"Unfortunately it's no longer your home," said Slick. He had used the word *home* instead of *house*, but neither Grace nor Huff had noticed. "The lender foreclosed and you didn't redeem within 6 weeks."

Grace looked puzzled and said, "I don't understand why you foreclosed, but we have 6 months to redeem the house."

"No," said Slick, "some lenders give you 6 months, but we only allow 6 weeks. You should have read the contract."

"You can only foreclose when the last one has left the home," said Grace. "Walter is still alive."

"Ah," said Slick, "that is a misunderstanding that many—I mean a few—persons have. Death is not the only way to leave the home. If a home owner permanently moves in with a relative or is permanently confined to a nursing home, that person has left the home."

"What about me?" asked Grace. "I am alive and still living here."

"Unfortunately, you do not qualify as a home owner," said Slick.

"I don't understand," said Grace.

"Have you read the deed to the property?" Slick asked Grace.

"Here, take a look," Slick said as he handed a copy of the deed to her. "The sole legal owner is your husband. Your name is not on it."

"Walter bought the house before we got married," Grace said. "I guess he never put my name on the deed."

"Unfortunate, but everyone has problems," said Slick, "which reminds me that I am going to be late for golf."

Huff walked to the TV, turned it on and suggested that Grace just relax for a bit. He and Slick got up to leave and Slick said that Grace could stay overnight and move out in the morning.

Grace had not been paying any attention to the TV or the advertisement then playing, but when she focused on the TV she heard "until the last one leaves the home." She finished her drink and threw the glass at the TV, aiming it at the head of that good looking son-of-a bitch she had listened to all these month.

<u>THE END</u>

CAMBRIDGE UNIVERSITY PRESS – Sellout to China

The scene is the four-story building which houses the almost 500-year old Cambridge University Press (the "Press"), the building itself not being anywhere near that old. Two middle-aged gentlemen are engaged in a serious discussion as to whether or not the Press should publish a recently submitted manuscript. The older gentleman has the look of a worn out professor with his out-of-date suit (frayed at the elbows), red bow tie and rows of wrinkles above his thick framed glasses. He speaks with authority and conviction. His associate, a few years younger, is more casually dressed and has been with the Press almost as long. They have learned long ago to roll with the punches and adjust to changing times in the world and at the Press. Their names were Mr. Kow and Mr. Tow, respectively. Mr. Kow and Mr. Tow were both distantly related to former Prime Minister Neville Chamberlain, although they did not advertise the fact.

"I say, Tow," what do you think of this book?" Kow said.

"Well, the Press has never published this type of book before," Tow said.

"Can't be too careful," Kow said. "Taking chances is not the motto of the Press."

"Not at all," Tow said.

"Nor the way to keep one's job," Kow said.

"Wouldn't be easy to find other employment at our age," Tow said. "Not that it's easy for anyone these days."

Kow looked at his pocket watch, then at Tow, about to suggest that they go to lunch, but was interrupted by a loud rap on the door. "Enter," he said, instead of *come in*—something he had picked up from a play in the West End Theatre District of London decades ago.

A DHL deliveryman came in and handed a package to Tow, who was closer to the door. "It's not addressed to me," Tow said.

"Nobody here except you guys," said the DHL driver. "I just need a signature so I can get rid of this package and go on my way. I got a schedule to keep. Don't matter to me who signs."

While Tow was thinking over the responsibility involved, Kow said, "I'll sign for it," and Tow expressed a sign of relief. Making decisions was not his first love.

Tow quickly handed the package to Kow, who said, "It's from Beijing." Tow looked puzzled and Kow said, "That's in China."

"I know Beijing is in China," Tow said, "but we don't know anyone in China and the package is not addressed to either of us."

"I think we're stuck with it," Kow said. He held the package to his ear and shook it gently.

"Be careful, it might be a bomb," Tow said as he backed away.

"Nonsense," said Kow. "The package is very light and I don't hear anything ticking inside. I'm going to open it right now or else we will be staring at a Chinese puzzle all day."

The package was wrapped in brown paper, sealed with brown mailing tape and was securely tied with string. It appeared to be from some official Chinese government agency. Kow found a pair of scissors and cut the string, then peeled off the outer brown wrapping and opened the box. Under the cushioning material he found a much smaller box, bright red in colour and made of sturdy material.

"Anything inside explaining what this is all about?" Tow asked.

Kow rummaged through the cushioning material before shaking his head no.

"That's a beautiful box," Tow said. "It would be a shame to rip it apart just to find out what's inside."

"You do want to know what's inside, don't you." Kow asked.

"Yes, and then we need to get back to work," Tow said.

"You mean after lunch," Kow said, as he pulled the top off the small red box to find its contents wrapped in tissue paper. Kow very carefully pulled away the tissue paper and found a Chinese fortune cookie inside.

"Is this a joke?" Tow asked.

"If it is, it's a very expense one," Kow said, looking at his watch. "If we want lunch, we had better hurry before they stop serving."

"Bring the fortune cookie along. Today is Thursday so they should have Chinese food, but they never have fortune cookies," Tow said. "How fortuitous this is."

"Are you trying to impress me with fancy sounding words," Kow asked.

"Just a bad habit from University days to make my essays longer and sound more academic," Tow said.

***

Kow and Tow rushed to order their food and then ate at a leisurely pace. They ordered sandwiches as there was no Chinese food left. They pushed their empty plates aside and pulled their cups of tea closer. Kow placed the red box on the table, removed the fortune cookie and placed it on a paper napkin.

"It's bigger than usual but they only sent one," Kow said. "Do you want to toss a shilling for it or split it in two?"

"It's rather small to share," said Tow. "Why don't you eat it and give me the fortune inside?"

"You're not allowed to bring your own food," said the voice of a passing student who was obviously not familiar with the word diet.

The student took a few steps, then turned and stared at Kow and Tow, so they left and took the fortune cookie back to their office.

***

Back in the office, Kow removed the fortune cookie from the red box, broke it in half and handed the fortune to Tow, who unraveled it—an extremely long, narrow piece of paper.

"I've never seen one that long," Kow said. "Read it to me."

"One side merely says 'A SUGGESTION' and the other side is quite lengthy," Tow said, who then read it aloud.

> IT WOULD BE AN EXCELLENT IDEA AS A FRIEND OF CHINA TO BLOCK ACCESS ON THE CAMBRIDGE UNIVERSITY PRESS WEBSITE TO OBJECTIONABLE ARTICLES FROM *THE CHINA QUARTERLY*. FOR YOUR CONVENIENCE ENCLOSED IS A LIST OF APPROXIMATELY 300 SUCH OFFENSIVE ARTICLES.

Kow looked puzzled; then took a closer look inside the small red box. With the help of a letter opener he scraped a piece of paper from the bottom of the box and unfolded it over and over until it became the size of an A4 sheet of paper. Printed on both sides, it no doubt contained the names of over 300 articles.

"What do we do now"? Tow asked. "It said it was only a suggestion."

"Bollocks. It did not say it was *only* a suggestion; it said it was a suggestion," Kow said. "The meaning is rather obvious and we want continued access to the internet in China. Either we comply or suffer the consequences."

"We'll get a backlash from the academic community and be accused of enforcing censorship on behalf of Communist China if we agree to this," Tow said.

"Look, Apple, Bloomberg and Facebook are accommodating China in order to maintain access to the Chinese market," Kow said.

"Yes, but that's all about money," Tow said. "Who is responsible for making such an important decision anyway?"

"Unfortunately, we are," Kow said, "or rather, I am."

"I suppose you are right," Tow said, "but I am going to protest in my own small way."

"What are you going to do?" asked Kow.

"I am going to stop eating General Tso's chicken and egg foo young for one month," Tow said.

"Those are not really authentic Chinese dishes," Kow said.

"Doesn't matter," said Tow. "One month".

"Call the IT Department and have them send someone over straightaway to start removing access to the objectionable articles."

<u>THE END</u>

UK PUBLIC HEALTH & POLITICAL CORRECTNESS HEARINGS

The setting is a barge at Docklands near Canary Wharf in London, rocking gently in the River Thames as it waits for a tug boat to be hooked up. Something like a worn, prefabricated structure sits on the barge, which was previously used as a venue for a small theatre company—SUMMER THEATRE ON THE THAMES. The structure is filled with about forty persons of various description, age and ethnicity, some looking serious and others agitated. Today hearings will be held on the subject of political correctness. There is a difference of opinion as to which committee of Parliament should receive the report of these hearings. The choices are: (1) The Committee on Public Health and Diseases, or (2) The Committee on Universities and Free Speech.

Persons in attendance include a student union representative, one reporter, a few students and members of the public; they are seated in rows of wooden folding chairs from a previous era. At one end, the front for purposes of this temporary forum, is a long table that resembles a slab of wood resting on two sawhorses. Behind it are two chairs occupied by representatives of the Parliamentary Committees concerned and a chair in the center for the Chairman. At the end is an additional chair for the Clerk. On the wall behind the table is a hastily attached portrait of Her Majesty Queen Elizabeth II in a gold frame. There is a loud clunk, accompanied by a jolt as the barge connects to the tug boat and starts moving slowly along the Thames. The Clerk enters, followed by the Chairman, who heads for the chair in the center. They are both wearing black suits, the Chairman dressed for court except for his wig.

CLERK: All rise … except Jeremy Corbyn.

CHAIRMAN: I don't think he is here.

(Everyone, except Jeremy Corbyn, who is not present, stands)

CHAIRMAN: That's not necessary. Please be seated.

MP BIDDLECOMBE: It's about time we got started. I was beginning to get seasick just sitting here, rocking back and forth. It doesn't pay to be on time.

REPORTER (standing): I have a question.

CLERK: Questions will be taken in due course, when permitted by the Chairman.

REPORTER: I just want to know why this hearing is being held in the middle of the River Thames.

CLERK: I am not privy to that information.

LORD STRONG: We wanted to limit the number of persons in attendance to minimize costs.

REPORTER: Looks like you are trying to keep out demonstrators.

LORD STRONG: Not at all.

CLERK: Sounds like a good idea to me.

REPORTER: I wasn't addressing you.

(There is a murmur in the audience and the CHAIRMAN bangs a gavel several times)

REPORTER: Another thing, these seats are most uncomfortable.

LORD STRONG (to REPORTER): If you are unhappy you are free to leave.

REPORTER: How can I leave? We are in the middle of a river.

CLERK: What's that got to do with it? You can walk the plank.

REPORTER: I have never been so insulted.

CLERK: Hard to believe.

CHAIRMAN (to CLERK): Kindly apologize to the REPORTER.

CLERK: I apologize, as the barge has no plank, but we do have life vests and large inner tubes from lorries.

LORD STRONG (to REPORTER): Well, are you staying or leaving?

(The REPORTER sits in his *uncomfortable* chair)

CHAIRMAN (to CLERK): Proceed.

CLERK: Today's hearing is about whether political correctness unreasonably restricts free speech.

LORD STRONG: You mean suffocates free speech.

CHAIRMAN: You may express your viewpoint later.

MP BIDDLECOME: Seems to me that the first order of business is which of two Committees of Parliament should receive our findings. One view is that political correctness is an infringement of free speech and stifles ideas so the Committee on Universities and Free Speech is the correct one. The other view is that political correctness is a rapidly spreading disease which should be regulated by the Public Health and Disease Services.

STUDENT (standing): I object because you failed to give a "trigger warning."

MP BIDDLECOME: What are you talking about?

STUDENT (shaking nervously): You know, a trigger warning, that you are going to mention something that I might find offensive or make me feel uncomfortable.

MP BIDDLECOME: What kind of codswallop is that?

LORD STRONG: It's some kind of political correctness twaddle from the States that unfortunately has been endorsed by a majority of universities in the UK.

CHAIRMAN (to STUDENT): What was said that upset you?

STUDENT: The word "disease."

LORD STRONG (to STUDENT): Haven't you ever been sick?

STUDENT: I am also sensitive to that word.

MP BIDDLECOME: The word disease is no doubt going to be repeated many times. As a matter of fact, we are going to discuss whether or not political correctness is a disease. Why don't you just cover your ears?

STUDENT: If I cover both ears I cannot take notes.

MP BIDDLECOME: We all have problems, but they probably don't teach you how to deal with problems at university nowadays—just about retreating to safe spaces—where you can cuddle-up far away from the big, bad world.

LORD STRONG: I read that some of these safe spaces have cookies, stuffed animals, calming music, pillows, coloring books, games and toys—even Playdough.

MP BIDDLECOME: Another asinine idea that seems to have drifted over here from the States.

STUDENT: I again object to not being given a trigger warning.

CHAIRMAN: It's a little too late for that, and we are not obligated to do so in any event.

STUDENT: Then, I insist on being provided with a safe space while the current topic is discussed.

MP BIDDLECOME: Your bargaining position is not very good – out in the middle of the Thames.

LORD STRONG (to STUDENT): I believe that the only solution we can suggest is for you to cover your ears unless you want to leave, assuming that you know how to swim.

CHAIRMAN: I'm afraid that option is not available. It's illegal for anyone to swim in the Thames without prior permission from the Port of London Authority, at least between Crossness in east London and Putney Bridge in south-west London.

LORD STRONG (to STUDENT): I assume that you have a mobile phone. Would you like to call the Port of London Authority for permission?

STUDENT: Of course not.

MP BIDDLECOME (to STUDENT): I think we may be able to accommodate you. Why don't you wait in the men's toilet until we finish. If you put the seat down it shouldn't be any more uncomfortable than the chairs out here. The space is not very big, but there's a small window you can open if the smell is too much for you.

LORD STRONG: Of course, if someone knocks on the door you will have to let them in to piss or take a crap, maybe for a minute or two, or possibly longer. You never know.

STUDENT: I am used to a much more comfortable safe space than you are offering me. I will definitely report this to the National Union of Students.

LORD STRONG: You can report it to the *Sun* or the *Daily Express* as far as I'm concerned.

STUDENT: Those are some of the newspapers banned at my university.

LORD STRONG: More evidence of political correctness stifling free speech. Universities are supposed to be about learning, free exchanges of ideas and debates. They are turning into day care centers.

MP BIDDLECOME: I am sure there are some other students in the audience. Do any of you have a teddy bear that you can loan this STUDENT to keep him company in the toilet and help relieve his emotional stress?

(A female GRADUATE STUDENT comes forward and hands her teddy bear to the STUDENT who holds it tightly)

GRADUATE STUDENT: I only have one more term to finish my PhD; I never would have made it this far without my Teddy.

(The GRADUATE STUDENT pats Teddy on the head, then the STUDENT, and returns to her seat in the back)

MP BIDDLECOME: Very nice gesture.

GRADUATE STUDENT (to STUDENT): Oh, don't leave the window open all the way; I don't want Teddy to come down with anything.

LORD STRONG: I don't know if there is any toilet paper in the loo. Take your notepad with you, just in case.

(The STUDENT reluctantly walks over to the toilet, opens the door and pulls the light switch string once, then again and again. After being advised of the problem, MP BIDDLECOME calls over to the STUDENT that the barge hasn't been used for several months and no one remembered to replace the light bulbs. The STUDENT puts the seat down, opens the window and closes the door)

CHAIRMAN: Getting back to business, the choice of Committee will be deferred. I don't think that we can properly decide the most appropriate Committee until all of the issues have been discussed.

MP BIDDLECOME: Agreed. May I make an opening statement?

CHAIRMAN: Proceed.

MP BIDDLECOME: Ladies and Gentlemen.

REPORTER (interrupting): You can't say that any more.

MP BIDDLECOME: Why not?

REPORTER: The TfL has issued a new prohibition against saying "Ladies and Gentlemen" on public transport.

LORD STRONG: Bollocks. It reinforces the need to hold these hearings.

MP BIDDLECOME: In addition to being the dumbest thing I ever heard, we are not on public transport.

LORD STRONG: Furthermore, the TfL has no jurisdiction over these Parliamentary hearings.

CHAIRMAN: That is correct.

MP BIDDLECOME (to the CHAIRMAN): May I continue?

CHAIRMAN: Proceed.

MP BIDDLECOME: Ladies and gentlemen … excluding a certain member of the press … I wish to emphasize the importance of today's hearings. Professors have been ostracized and speakers prohibited from appearing on university campuses in increasing numbers for trying to present points of view that do not agree with University officials or more often the objections of student unions. Newspapers, books, songs and words are banned and students are expelled based on mere allegations that their views are controversial. Emotion now governs over reason, with universities quickly caving into the latest moaning of ultra-liberal students coddled from birth. Maoist conformity is enforced with student codes of conduct and student unions dictating the establishment of elaborately furnished safe spaces with the most coddling amenities.

LORD STRONG: These restrictive policies and actions are not limited to on-campus activities or speech, but extend to extra-curricular student political and social activities. Students and university staff are encouraged to report what other students or professors say on Twitter. This is reminiscent of Nazi Germany where each block of apartments had a *Block Warden* whose duties included spying on fellow citizens and reporting them to the government about any unfavorable comments about the regime. Even friends, neighbors and family members reported each other to the Gestapo. If this trend continues, the only thing missing will be the brown shirts and jackboots.

MP BIDDLECOME: I have with me a copy of a recent *Free Speech University Rankings*, a "spiked project" that analyzed campus censorship on 115 UK universities. It found that 63.5% of them actively censor speech and 30.5% stifle speech through excessive regulation, based on the policies of the universities and students' unions. This brings to mind the "Thought Police" in George Orwell's *Nineteen Eighty-Four* (1984), where individualism was persecuted and unapproved thoughts, speech and actions were crimes.

CHAIRMAN: I can see that the Committee on Universities and Free Speech is the proper committee to receive our report of this hearing.

MP BIDDLECOME: Maybe so, but political correctness may also equally be viewed as a rapidly spreading disease, which unchecked will impede the minds of students and destroy their ability to think and reason. The well-known American comedian George Carlin is reported to have said that political correctness is fascism pretending to be manners, but I prefer to say that political correctness is merely a euphemism for censorship. Some of the tactics and policies are nothing less that mind control. This is a matter to be regulated by the Public Health and Disease Services.

LORD STRONG: Another aspect concerning public health and the spread of disease recently occurred at Strathclyde University after cleaning staff complained about encountering poo in bins and showers, as well as finding used toilet paper where it shouldn't be. A memo sent out to the University's multicultural population stating that although different countries have different practices, the accepted practice in the UK was to use the WC, was disowned by the University after it received a substantial backlash from students who were offended.

MINORITY STUDENT (standing, in a loud voice): Damn right; it was insulting. I come from a country where several hundred million people take a shit outdoors everyday—helps fertilize the crops too.

MP BIDDLECOME: I think that you will find the UK quite green as a result of frequent rain, rather than people shitting outdoors everywhere. Moreover, our local councils require dog walkers to carry plastic bags and clean up dog poop.

MINORITY STUDENT: You won't even find the words *toilet paper* in our language, or the dictionary for that matter.

MP BIDDLECOME: You might do your fellow students in the UK a favor by inventing such a translation in your country's language.

LORD STRONG: Be that as it may, you have to make some adjustments to your lifestyle when you live in a foreign country. For example, you cannot graduate from a UK university if you cannot write or speak English. Furthermore, hygiene and sanitation are matters of public concern that prevent the spread of disease.

MP BIDDLECOME: I believe that Strathclyde University is in the process of reaching a compromise with its cleaning staff, which has resulted in the following proposed policy:

> Effective immediately all staff and students are free to piss or take a crap anywhere on university premises. In order to respect certain cultures, men will be allowed to shit in the university swimming pool only on Monday, Wednesday and Friday—women may relieve themselves in the pool on Tuesday, Thursday and Saturday. The pool will necessarily be closed on Sundays for extensive cleaning.

CHAIRMAN: I think our report is equally important to the Public Health and Disease Services because of the corrupting effect that political correctness has on poisoning the minds of students rather than poo at Strathclyde University.

LORD STRONG: There is a much bigger health problem than poo at Strathclyde University

CLERK: Especially if you step in it.

CHAIRMAN: You need not state the obvious.

CLERK: It's even worse when you slip on it. You could end up stinking up the inside of an ambulance.

MP BIDDLECOME: You sound like you are speaking from personal experience.

CLERK: As a matter of fact ….

CHAIRMAN: I'm sure that it's an interesting story, but some other time, if you please.

LORD STRONG: As I was about to say, we need to be concerned about the mental health of students. Apparently many of these mollycoddled students are truly distressed at hearing anything the least bit contrary to their views. This may result in psychological problems with long-term effects.

MP BIDDLECOME: That is certainly something for the Public Health and Disease Services to consider. Even the words *free speech* or *democracy* will throw some hypersensitive students into a tizzy.

CHAIRMAN: Another negative aspect of political correctness is rewriting history, something that authoritarian regimes the world over have done repeatedly.

LORD STRONG: Or erasing history, such as the protests to remove the statute of Cecil Rhodes at the entrance of the

Rhodes Building at Oriel College, Oxford. Some African student started a big brouhaha to remove the statute after helping himself to the benefits of a Rhodes scholarship.

MP BIDDLECOME: Biting the hand that feeds you—kind of like modern day cannibalism.

LORD STRONG: Interesting analogy, but I wouldn't go quite that far. It does seem quite hypocritical though.

MP BIDDLECOME: If their point is that the money to build Oriel College was stolen from Africa, should we tear down the Rhodes Building and ship the stones and bricks to South Africa? They could build a mausoleum celebrating the death of free speech.

LORD STRONG: Maybe the scholarship money should be repaid to Oriel College by the ungrateful, offended recipients and then sent on to South Africa.

CHAIRMAN: Let's move on. In this age of conformity and snowflake insanity another danger is the well-entrenched practice to dis-invite or prohibit speakers from appearing on university campuses, including men and women who are well-respected in their profession, if any overly sensitive student or group of campus censors protests that they would be uncomfortable, although speakers promoting anarchy are welcome. Others who do make it on campus are shouted down at the slightest improper comment.

LORD STRONG: As political correctness sweeps across university campuses in the States and the UK, students are constantly being brainwashed and bullied. It's not only speech but behavior that is being regulated by the political correctness brigade. Professors are being bullied online by students who are easily offended by opposing views. This is criminal but you are not going to get any convictions.

CHAIRMAN: I think we have finished talking about disease and sickness. Maybe we should advise the snowflake in the toilet that he can come back now.

(The CLERK, after being directed by the CHAIRMAN, goes over to the men's toilet and knocks on the door. The door opens and the STUDENT comes out holding his notebook in one hand and the Teddy Bear in the other. The GRADUATE STUDENT rushes over to reclaim Teddy. She wrinkles her nose, sniffs Teddy)

STUDENT: I'm sorry but we had an accident. When I reached up to close the window I slipped and Teddy fell into the toilet. There wasn't any water in it but it does smell a bit funny.

(The GRADUATE STUDENT, wearing a T-shirt which says "Peace & Love" slaps the STUDENT in the face and returns to her seat. The shocked STUDENT turns to go back inside the toilet, reconsiders and takes a different seat on the end of a row of mostly empty chairs)

MP BIDDLECOME: We should discuss the obsession by students and capitulating universities with the recent trivial nonsense called "cultural appropriation."

LORD STRONG: What the bloody hell is that?

MP BIDDLECOME: In a nutshell it's moaners from other countries who complain that food served by UK colleges misrepresents their culture. Pembroke College, Cambridge recently came under attack by students complaining that it was serving culturally insensitive food.

LORD STRONG: No doubt another fad started in the States.

MP BIDDLECOME: Yes, apparently started by the student Stasi in the States condemning the action of a person from one culture who borrows something from another culture.

CARIBBEAN STUDENT: This is a serious problem—serving a fake dish called Jamaican Stew. It doesn't even have the right ingredients—beef and mangos—to be authentic.

UNIVERSITY COOK (to CARIBBEAN STUDENT): Can you list the ingredients in my Jamaican Stew or give me a complete recipe of an authentic Jamaican Stew?

CARIBBEAN STUDENT: Not off of the top of my head, but I know when it tastes right.

UNIVERSITY COOK: Have you ever spent more than ten minutes in a kitchen or cooked any Jamaican food yourself?

CARIBBEAN STUDENT: Course not, my Mom does the cooking.

UNIVERSITY COOK: So you have no clue how to make Jamaican Stew. Let me tell you something, there is no official recipe for it. When you go back to Jamaica, visit ten different restaurants or ten different family homes and you will find that each one makes Jamaican Stew a bit differently even though most of the ingredients are the same.

CARIBBEAN STUDENT: Who says I'm going back?

CLERK: Sounds like a good idea to me.

UNIVERSITY COOK: I got online to search for recipes and found dozens of recipes for Jamaican Stew—some using the term "authentic." The one which I selected just happened to use beef and mangos. We try to make food for students more interesting by providing a variety of dishes from around the world.

CARIBBEAN STUDENT: That's not the way I see it.

UNIVERSITY COOK: You don't have to eat what we serve. You could bring your own sandwiches, but you probably don't even know how to make one. Many students have eaten our Jamaican Stew and everyone seems to like it, except for you and two other moaners—probably friends of yours—who are too lazy to furnish us with a so-called more authentic recipe.

LORD STRONG: It's about bringing cultures together, not appropriating cultures. Only an extremely naive person would think that all of these recipes from around the world were 100% authentic, especially in a university café or food hall. Although the food of a particular country may generally be described as spicy or bland, how can there be a single authentic recipe for a particular dish? Even if ingredients are similar there will be countless variations of any recipe depending on individual cooks, families or geographic regions within the same country.

CHAIRMAN: In a way, claiming that an item on a menu is authentic is like puffery—advertising or making representations relying on exaggeration or superlatives to make things sound better—such as the best pizza in Shoreditch. Such statements are based on subjective rather than objective opinions and most consumers do not take them seriously.

MP BIDDLECOME: There was an article recently in one of the liberal newspapers by some bore claiming that barbeque is a form of cultural power and that by eating it you are insulting Africans.

LORD STRONG: Bollocks. What does this clown want the government to do—close down all restaurants serving foods from other countries? No more Chinese, French, Italian, Greek, Japanese or Indian restaurants or pizza parlors in the UK? In addition to the stupidity of so-called cultural appropriation, look how many jobs would be lost and small businesses closed down because of a few easily offended bozos.

MP BIDDLECOME: There is probably at least one Chinese restaurant in almost every city in the world. Should all of them be closed down except for the ones in China? They are run by Chinese owners, and many of the dishes have been westernized to suit customer taste.

LORD STRONG: I would be hard pressed to find that cultural appropriation, and certainly not racist.

CHAIRMAN: This cultural appropriation nonsense extends to much more than food. One student union at the University of East Anglia stopped a restaurant from handing out Sombreros to students. A university in Canada even wanted yoga classes cancelled because it considered them cultural appropriation.

LORD STRONG: Looks like it is better to be politically correct than healthy in Canada, not that I would ever go there.

MP BIDDLECOME: Racism is used blatantly as justification for political correctness. The latest example of this insanity comes from Oxford University. The university's Equality and Diversity Unit recently lectured students in a newsletter that if they avoided eye contact when speaking to another person they were guilty of the crimes of subtle racism and racial micro-aggression, no doubt felonies worthy of incarceration in the Tower of London if they had their way.

STUDENT UNION REP: You are not taking cultural appropriation seriously, especially as it concerns food, which affects minority students more than other types of appropriation.

MP BIDDLECOME: What university does your student union represent?

STUDENT UNION REP: I'm not required to answer that.

LORD STRONG: Afraid of your own shadow are you?

(Suddenly there is a commotion in the back of the room. A young GIRL WITH GLASSES screams as something jumps out of her backpack, which had been sitting on the floor beside her chair. It is a small white rabbit intent on not being caught and returned to the backpack. The rabbit runs back and forth, then up to the front until cornered under the table)

MP BIDDLECOME: This is outrageous. What is a rabbit doing here?

GIRL WITH GLASSES: It's my comfort animal. I take him everywhere.

(She finally scoops up the rabbit and holds it close to her body)

LORD STRONG: I hope your rabbit is not going to poop on the floor. We have to return the barge in the same condition. Did you bring a plastic bag—just in case?

(The GIRL WITH GLASSES does not answer, just talks quietly to her rabbit and returns to her seat, still holding the rabbit instead of returning it to the backpack. A few of those nearby go over to see the cute little rabbit. The CHAIRMAN bangs his gavel several times)

CHAIRMAN: Please return to your seats. We have serious matters to discuss.

MP BIDDLECOME: I believe the STUDENT UNION REP was about to say something.

STUDENT UNION REP: Definitely. You need to take cultural appropriation more seriously because many students are truly offended, especially about misrepresenting their native food.

LORD STRONG: Do you have any data to back up your claim?

STUDENT UNION REP: None that I care to disclose.

LORD STRONG: Do you have any suggestions as to what we should do, or just unverified complaints?

STUDENT UNION REP: You could start by banning culturally offensive food from university cafés and food halls.

LORD STRONG: How should we define culturally offensive food?

STUDENT UNION REP: Food from other cultures that isn't authentic.

LORD STRONG: How should authentic be defined—recipes with 100% customary ingredients or 90% or 85%? How low should the bar be? Many cooks at home and in restaurants do not measure the exact amount of each ingredient as they prepare food, so the amount varies from one time to the next.

STUDENT UNION REP: You're making this complicated.

LORD STRONG: Not at all. It was your idea, but it cannot be enforced without basic definitions. This requires thinking and making decisions, something you may not be familiar with. Food can't be outlawed merely because of a few alleged complaints.

MP BIDDLECOME: The university cooks also have rights. They are entitled to know with certainty what the rules are. Recipes would have to be compiled, probably from online searches, ingredients listed and compared to come up with an acceptable percentage for each one.

LORD STRONG (to STUDENT UNION REP): I know that you have a problem with answering questions, but I will ask one anyway. Do you only care about the ingredients if food is identified as being from a particular culture?

STUDENT UNION REP: I don't understand the question.

LORD STRONG: To make things as easy as humanly possible, let's try some examples. Would you object if Jamaican Stew based on your Mom's recipe were merely described as 'Today's Special' without disclosing the country of origin. Try to focus on the question. It is not based on failing to give your Mom credit, but on the question of cultural appropriation.

STUDENT UNION REP: I'm not sure; that's a tough one.

LORD STRONG: Let's try another one. How about pizza not made the way it is made in Italy—though each region of Italy has its own version of pizza—being described as 'Italian Pizza?'

STUDENT UNION REP: Not acceptable.

LORD STRONG: What about a westernized version of 'Chop Suey' prepared by a Chinese chef with his own recipe?

STUDENT UNION REP: That doesn't make it authentic Chinese food.

LORD STRONG: Fair enough.

MP BIDDLECOME: I don't know that I agree. If the Chop Suey is not described as an authentic Chinese dish, how is it cultural appropriation?

CHAIRMAN: I find it hard to call a westernized version of Chop Suey cultural appropriation if it is served in a restaurant in Chinatown that serves mostly authentic Chinese food.

MP BIDDLECOME: Seems to me that any determination of culturally insensitive food, if we were to agree to such a classification, should be based on the particular name used to describe the dish and the percentage of authentic ingredients, irrespective of the nationality of the cook.

STUDENT UNION REP: So, are you actually going to do something?

CHAIRMAN: The hearings will adjourn for fifteen minutes while the Committee considers what recommendations to include in its report.

(The three Committee members step outside for a much needed breath of fresh air and a smoke, deliberate for several minutes, and return to their seats)

CHAIRMAN: The Committee has decided what to discuss in its report. There are many issues about free speech, censorship, mental health, and the primary purposes of universities that must seriously be considered. Because the issues cannot be totally isolated from each other, our report will be submitted to both committees of Parliament—the Committee on Universities and Free Speech and the Public Health and Disease Services.

STUDENT UNION REP: What about cultural appropriation.

LORD STRONG: Cultural appropriation will be discussed in general terms and in more detail with respect to food from other cultures. In addition to the complaints from sensitive students, this raises the issue of possible false labelling or false advertising under the Consumer Protection from Unfair Trading Regulations.

MP BIDDLECOME: Those regulations apply to business-to-consumer transactions. I'm not sure they apply to universities or colleges.

LORD STRONG: Even so, who owns or manages cafés or food halls on or near campuses might be relevant.

CHAIRMAN: Our report will also be sent to the Office of Fair Trade. They can decide who their regulations apply to and if there are any violations.

CLERK: Your report should also recommend prohibiting any of those crazy recipes from California.

MP BIDDLECOME: Thank you for your input, but are you again speaking from personal experience?

CHAIRMAN: Let's move on and finish this hearing.

STUDENT UNION REP: I didn't hear anything about what specific actions you are going to take to prevent cultural misappropriation of food from other cultures.

LORD STRONG: If you would be more patient, probably not your greatest strength, you will eventually find out. The only *action* that we are going to take is to report the issues discussed here today and our recommendations, which will be forwarded to the appropriate Committees of Parliament and government authorities for consideration.

STUDENT UNION REP: So, when will your new rules to prohibit cultural appropriation take effect?

LORD STRONG (to MP BIDDLECOME): Did I say anything about this Committee issuing any rules?

MP BIDDLECOME: No—only recommendations, not rules.

CLERK: I didn't hear anything about rules either—only recommendations.

LORD STRONG: Thank you once again for your input.

STUDENT UNION REP: I'm still waiting for details.

MP BIDDLECOME: If we were to make any specific recommendations in our written report, they would be subject to review by the respective committees. Any restrictions on food would have to apply to cafés, restaurants, food halls, pizza parlors and takeaway establishments that are located on any accredited university or college or maybe within ten kilometers to be meaningful.

LORD STRONG (to STUDENT UNION REP): I'm sure that we could count on you to measure distances for compliance.

CLERK: I assume that distance would be as the crow flies.

LORD STRONG: You assume correctly.

MP BIDDLECOME: If I may continue, preferably without further interruption, I will ask if anyone here thinks that the following foods should be prohibited for not being culturally authentic – Belgian waffles, Chop Suey, French toast, Greek salad, Hungarian goulash, Irish stew, Pizza, Schnitzel, Swedish meatballs, Swiss steak and Tandoori chicken.

CHINESE STUDENT: You can't do that. My parents own a small Chinese restaurant bordering my college and I work there part-time to help pay off my tuition loans. Chop Suey is our biggest seller.

STUDENT UNION REP: You didn't list BBQ.

GRADUATE STUDENT: Now you are going too far. You can't prohibit my favorite food.

STUDENT UNION REP: The student union will decide for you which foods should be banned as culturally insensitive.

GRADUATE STUDENT: You are an arrogant jackass as well as a fascist.

ANOTHER STUDENT: How am I going to stay alive without hot pizza in the afternoon and cold pizza leftovers in the morning? I'm feeling insecure already.

MP BIDDLECOME (to LORD STRONG): Sounds like some backlash to political correctness and Maoist conformity.

LORD STRONG: A nice sound indeed.

MP BIDDLECOME: And about time.

CHAIRMAN (banging his gavel): This hearing is adjourned.

(Everyone is jolted as the barge bumps into the dock from where the journey started. The rabbit jumps from the arms of the GIRL WITH GLASSES and the chase begins anew)

THE END

WHO's GONNA FIX MY TOILET?

The gathering at the Senator's beach-front second home on the exclusive island of Palm Beach, Florida, was well attended by the elite and their children who were recent university graduates. Outside on the veranda one could hear the sound of the waves and feel the invigorating wind, which helped refresh those who had consumed one too many, or maybe more than one too many. Inside, the proud parents of the recent graduates were trying to impress each other with the spectacular accomplishments of their little darlings. Even though the doors to the veranda were open, the air inside was full of endless bullshit. Conversations could be heard between various couples trying to outdo each other.

BELINDA: You know—my Harper will be going to study medicine at Johns Hopkins University in the fall. He's going to be a doctor.

NEVILLE: Congratulations. The tuition is rather expensive but I'm sure that you can afford it.

BELINDA: It's not going to cost me anything.

NEVILLE: Scholarship?

BELINDA: No. We are loaning Harper the money; he'll have to pay us back after he starts his medical practice.

NEVILLE: How unusual.

BELINDA: You don't stay rich by pissing away your money.

NEVILLE: I guess not, but he will have to specialize in the right field to pay you back during your lifetime.

BELINDA: I think urologists make good money.

NEVILLE: If you like sticking your gloved finger up someone's ass all day long.

BELINDA: Oh dear, my Harper wouldn't like that. Your son is a dentist, isn't he?

NEVILLE: Yes.

BELINDA: I'm sure dentists do okay but not anyway near what a surgeon can earn.

NEVILLE: General surgeons don't make top dollar. You have got to specialize in the right thing.

BELINDA: Such as?

NEVILLE: Right now there is a severe shortage of surgeons who specialise in left elbow injuries.

BELINDA: You're kidding, right?

NEVILLE: Not at all.

BELINDA: Doesn't sound very exciting.

NEVILLE: $500,000 a year isn't exciting?

BELINDA: Oh, that's different.

NEVILLE: Lots of millionaire golfers need this kind of surgery—they're always having problems.

(Someone waives to NEVILLE from across the room and he waives back)

NEVILLE (continuing): Excuse me, but there's someone I need to talk to.

(BELINDA drops her glass of champagne as a young man—ALFRED—bumps into her. He has obviously had too much to drink)

ALFRED: Where's the toilet?

BELINDA: You could say sorry.

ALFRED: Yeah, sure, sorry, but I don't feel well. I need the toilet, like now.

BELINDA: Up the stairs, first door on the right.

(ALFRED works his way up the circular staircase, holding on to the railing for dear life. Across the room NEVILLE and his friend KENDRICK chat for a while, have a good laugh and KENDRICK crosses the room to BELINDA)

KENDRICK: What happened to you? Your gown is all wet.

BELINDA: Your son ALFRED bumped into me; he's drunk.

KENDRICK: Sorry about that.

BELINDA: What's he going to do now?

KENDRICK: Law school.

BELINDA: Any school that I might have heard of?

KENDRICK: ALFRED is going to study Global Health Law at Georgetown University and then at the Graduate Institute of International and Development Studies in Geneva.

BELINDA: I suppose he will specialise in some area.

KENDRICK: Medical malpractice.

BELINDA: That's not a very nice occupation. My son's going to be a doctor.

KENDRICK: What are the odds they will end up on opposite sides in court? ALFRED is going to specialise in a new field that's really hot right now.

BELINDA: What might that be?

KENDRICK: Suing the pants off doctors who specialise in surgery on the left elbow for malpractice.

(They are standing adjacent to the staircase and suddenly realise that they are standing in a puddle of water. Looking up they see water flowing down the staircase. ALFRED makes his way down the stairs and once at the bottom slips and falls to the floor)

ALFRED: Sorry about the flood.

(The water gradually seeps across the floor and the guests start backing away. The SENATOR rushes over and looks at ALFRED)

SENATOR: What happened?

ALFRED: A roll of toilet paper got stuck in the toilet and it started overflowing. I kept trying to flush the toilet but the handle broke off. Here!

(ALFRED gives the handle to the SENATOR, who gives it to a waiter)

SENATOR: Excuse me. I must call a plumber.

(The SENATOR makes his way across the wet floor to a small writing desk and thumbs through a telephone book looking for a plumber, finds only four in Palm Beach and the surrounding area)

SENATOR: I don't believe it. There used to be several pages advertising plumbing services.

(The SENATOR dials one number, then another and another)

CALL 1 - AUTOMATED VOICE MAIL: We are now closed for vacation and will reopen …

CALL 2 - AUTOMATED VOICE MAIL: Press 1 for English; 2 for Spanish; 3 for Haitian; 4 for French; or 5 to leave a message.

CALL 3 - AUTOMATED VOICE MAIL: This number is no longer in service. Have a nice day.

CALL 4 (answered by JERRY): Yeah. Kind of late to be calling.

SENATOR: I need a plumber.

JERRY: I don't do that no more.

SENATOR (speaking loudly): It's an emergency.

JERRY: Take it easy, I got a hangover. I've been out celebrating because I just graduated.

SENATOR: Are you or are you not a plumber?

JERRY: Not really. I was working for my Dad part-time while going to vocational school to become a plumber, but the school went bust after the government offered free college tuition to everyone. I don't like getting my hands dirty anyway. I just graduated from culinary school.

SENATOR: What about your father? Don't tell me that he quit plumbing to go to college too?

JERRY: No, he died when he installed a faulty water heater and it exploded. My Mom sold the business to another plumber but he went out of business. Seems like all the older plumbers have died and the young ones all gone off to college thanks to the free tuition you got through Congress.

SENATOR: Who's gonna fix my toilet?

THE END

I'M ILLEGAL – I want my benefits

Some say that it all started when then Governor Jerry Brown declared California to be a "sanctuary state." Though he did not specify, this probably extended to the twelve mile limit off the shoreline. After that things only got worse, or better, depending on your point of view or which side of the gravy train you were on.

One of the welcoming signs at the United States-Tijuana border reads:

<u>WARNING!</u>

If you are entering the United States
without presenting yourself to an Immigration
SUPERVISOR,
YOU MAY BE ARRESTED AND PROSECUTED
for violating U.S. Immigration and Customs Laws.

A few yards further a large sign reads (with a corresponding sign in Spanish below):

WELCOME TO THE GREAT SANCTUARY STATE OF
CALIFORNIA

No visa, no problem
No ID, no problem
No money, no problem
No food or water, no problem
No transportation – visit our VIP Center

Just past the welcome sign is a smaller sign (in Spanish only) announcing the VIP Center. Inside, the following amenities are offered without charge, curtesy of the

Governor of the Great Sanctuary State of California: bottled water, beer, sandwiches, tacos and Starbucks coffee. On one side are clean toilets and on the far side is a window to sign up for free limo service to a nearly immigration lawyer. In between are padded sofas and chairs and small tables. Toys for small children are scattered about.

A sign inside (in Spanish only) reads:

Unlike rumours that you may have heard the streets in the United States, even in Hollywood, are not paved with gold. However, if you remain in California everything is free. If you are here illegally you are given priority and go to the front of the line.

Farther north, Los Angeles to be exact, HORACE was riding his bicycle, texting on his iPhone so intently that he did not notice the pickup truck that suddenly swerved to avoid a large pothole. The truck looked as it had been rescued from the junk yard some time ago and had lawn mowing equipment in the back. The truck climbed the curb and came to a sudden stop, throwing the driver against the front window. One of the lawn mowers fell out of the back and into the path of HORACE and his bike. When they had recovered, HORACE and the TRUCK DRIVER started cursing each other, the former in English and the latter in Spanish. Horace had no idea what the other guy was saying as his Spanish was limited to a few words—tacos, tortillas, guacamole, tequila, and cerveza.

They were both taken to the nearest hospital in separate ambulances. HORACE arrived first, followed by the TRUCK DRIVER several minutes later. They each registered at the emergency desk and were told to wait. The two glared at each other for twenty-seven minutes until the

TRUCK DRIVER was taken inside. HORACE protested that he got there and signed in first but was informed that undocumented workers (a euphemism for illegal aliens in HORACE'S opinion) came first as the Great Sanctuary State of California wanted to make them feel welcome, and no doubt looked upon them as future voters. HORACE was also told that he should consider himself lucky as this hospital was designated as a trauma center, which usually meant a wait of several hours because of the high volume of drug addicts and gun-shot wounds which had priority. After being treated for his injuries, which were minor, HORACE was handed a form to submit to his insurance company.

HORACE didn't have an actual insurance policy and had collected some money when he was a student from California's version of Medicaid, known as Medi-Cal as he was then below 138% of the federal poverty level. He went to the local Medi-Cal office and waited his turn. When called, HORACE went to window number 4 and turned toward the person in line at window number 3—the TRUCK DRIVER. They gave each other a brief stare before turning their attention to the clerks behind their respective windows. HORACE was asked a few questions, including his place of work, income and education.

CLERK: I am sorry that you no longer qualify for benefits under Medi-Cal.

HORACE: What do you mean I don't qualify?

CLERK: Your income is too high.

HORACE: What are you talking about? My income is below the poverty level, even less than last time.

CLERK: Once you have graduated we use your potential income based on your university, degree and major.

HORACE: That is ridiculous. Since I graduated it seems like nobody is hiring college or university graduates. I've been looking for six months and all I can get is a part-time job at a grocery store. The only skill they require is to be able to say "paper or plastic."

(HORACE looks to his left and sees the clerk at window 3 give the TRUCK DRIVER a hand full of $100 bills)

HORACE (continuing): I don't believe it. That's the guy who ran into me with his truck. The clerk gave him a lot of cash and I know for a fact that he's here illegally. It's not fair.

CLERK: That doesn't matter. Undocumented workers are now entitled to benefits under Medi-Cal. Too bad you are not in the Great Sanctuary State of California illegally.

(HORACE walks to the nearest bar, orders a beer, then another, all the time thinking about what the CLERK had said: "Too bad you are not in the Great Sanctuary State of California illegally."

HORACE (to himself): Well, that was the solution.

(The next day HORACE goes to the Medi-Cal office, waits until the CLERK goes to lunch and another takes his place; then he approaches the window and presents his claim again)

NEW CLERK: I see from the file that you were here yesterday and your claim was denied.

HORACE: I didn't get to explain all the facts.

NEW CLERK: There's nothing I can do. You will have to speak with a SUPERVISOR.

HORACE: Fine.

NEW CLERK: Wait here.

(The NEW CLERK walks away and returns in a few minutes. He comes around the counter and motions for HORACE to follow him to the office of a SUPERVISOR. HORACE waits outside the door while the NEW CLERK hands the claim to the SUPERVISOR and talks briefly to her)

SUPERVISOR: Now you are claiming that you are entitled to medical benefits because you are in the United States illegally. How is that possible?

HORACE: My birth certificate says that I was born in Hawaii, but everyone knows that Hawaiian birth certificates can be forged. I was actually born in Kenya.

SUPERVISOR: Really. Why did you leave?

HORACE: It's a long story.

SUPERVISOR: Then you had better step on it because the office closes at four o'clock.

HORACE (looking at the wall clock): Ten minutes should be enough time.

SUPERVISOR: You only have five minutes. I am allowed by union rules to be at the front door by four o'clock.

HORACE: No problem. I got into a spot of trouble by making a comment about President Buhari of Kenya.

SUPERVISOR: Buhari is President of Nigeria, not Kenya.

HORACE: Is that so. Maybe he moved?

SUPERVISOR: Your story smells fishy.

HORACE: Well, let me explain. You see …

SUPERVISOR (standing): Time's up. I'm outta here.

HORACE: I'll be back.

SUPERVISOR: Don't bother; you'll be denied again.

(The next morning HORACE takes a bus to the Ecuadorian Consulate on Wilshire Boulevard. He would have preferred the Ecuadorian Embassy but Washington, D.C. was too far away. After a short wait HORACE moves forward and sits in a chair in front of a desk. He is carrying a large duffle bag which he places on the floor next to the desk)

CONSULATE EMPLOYEE: What can I do for you?

HORACE: I am seeking political asylum.

CONSULATE EMPLOYEE: On what basis?

HORACE: I am in the United States illegally.

CONSULATE EMPLOYEE: Where were you born?

HORACE: Venice.

CONSULATE EMPLOYEE: Let me write that down—Venice, Italy.

HORACE: No. Venice, California.

CONSULATE EMPLOYEE: How can you be in the United States illegally if you were born here?

HORACE: I have renounced my United States citizenship. I am in the United States illegally because I have no visa.

CONSULATE EMPLOYEE: When did you do that?

(HORACE puts the duffle bag on his lap, pulls out a letter and hands it to the CONSULATE EMPLOYEE, who reads it carefully)

CONSULATE EMPLOYEE: Is this letter a copy?

HORACE: No, it's the original. I am asking you to deliver it to the United States Government on my behalf.

CONSULATE EMPLOYEE: Even if we did that, it would probably not be effective for a while and certainly not until it is received and processed by the proper department of the United States Government.

HORACE: No problem. I am prepared to wait here until all the paperwork is taken care of.

(HORACE pats the duffle bag)

CONSULATE EMPLOYEE: What's in the bag?

HORACE: My belongings, so I can sleep here.

CONSULATE EMPLOYEE: We do not provide such services.

HORACE: Why not? You've been putting up that freeloader in the Ecuadorian Embassy in London for several years

CONSULATE EMPLOYEE: We have a new President in Ecuador who wants to get rid of him.

HORACE: I won't be here that long and I'll be a much better guest because I don't even own a cat to shit all over your carpet. Well, what is your answer?

CONSULATE EMPLOYEE: Out.

(The CONSULATE EMPLOYEE comes around the desk, picks up the duffle bag and tosses it outside the entrance. There is the sound of glass breaking as the duffle bag lands.

HORACE: You broke my French Press. How am I going to make coffee here every morning?

(HORACE rushes outside to inspect the contents of his duffle bag. His foot is injured as the door is slammed shut and locked)

HORACE (to himself): Now I need another trip to the hospital and then to the Medi-Cal office. I need a new strategy—maybe buy some fake ID in McArthur Park near downtown Los Angeles, but I need Mexican documents, not American. If not, maybe I can swap my U.S. ID with someone for his Mexican ID. If that doesn't work …

<u>THE END</u>

GET THE PRESIDENT – DOJ Black Book

The scene is a converted office above a shoe repair shop in Georgetown, Washington, D.C. The sign on the office door says PRIVATE. The inside is divided into a small kitchenette, washroom, small interview—interrogation—room and a large office. The contents disclose the age of the rooms and their furnishings. At one end sits a large desk, behind it an imposing chair, and in front two less imposing chairs. On the wall behind the desk is a black and white photo of J. Edgar Hoover—long-time Director of the FBI. A large conference table lined with chairs occupies the center of the room. At the other end of the room is a long, leather sofa with two matching leather chairs, all rather tired looking. The "interview room" contains a small table and two chairs, the uncomfortable one obviously for "guests." On the wall facing the guest chair hangs a four by six foot poster of a dilapidated blue bus, with part of a human body protruding from underneath. Below it a caption reads "THIS COULD BE YOU." Next to it is a smaller poster of the Bobby Fuller Four musical group with the caption "I fought the law and the law won."

The office houses a clandestine planning center for the Department of Justice (DOJ), far removed from the official premises of the DOJ on Constitution Avenue and unknown to the FBI, so it is hoped. Although trusted FBI agents are used from time to time, they are never invited here. On the other side of town the SPECIAL COUNSEL is preparing to leave his office at the DOJ.

SPECIAL COUNSEL (looking at his watch): I won't be back this afternoon.

SECRETARY: Shall I call for your limousine?

SPECIAL COUNSEL: Yes. I'll be downstairs in five minutes.

(The SPECIAL COUNSEL is a tall serious looking man, always sporting an expensive suit and tie but never a smile. He instructs the driver to let him off in front of the AMC Theatres in Georgetown and walks up the green colored stone steps and enters the building, then washes his hands in the men's room and leaves. He walks up 31st Street and crosses over to Wisconsin Avenue and continues along the brick sidewalk before stopping in front of a shoe repair shop. A sign indicates that one should ring the bell for entry)

PROPRIETOR: May I help you?

SPECIAL COUNSEL: I wonder if you repair umbrellas.

PROPRIETOR: Yes, but only on Thursdays.

(They do the secret handshake, both satisfied. The PROPRIETOR leads the SPECIAL COUNSEL into a back room, unlocks a door and the SPECIAL COUNSEL walks up a set of stairs leading to the office. He pushes six numbers on the alarm system and enters. Across town, near the United States Capitol, another person prepares to journey to Georgetown)

ANOTHER SECRETARY: Shall I call for your limousine?

SENATOR: No, thank you. The weather is quite nice today, for a change. I think I will walk.

(The SENATOR leaves the Russel Senate Office Building and walks to the Union Station Metro and boards the red line for DuPont Circle where he takes a taxi to

Georgetown. He gets out two blocks from his destination and walks the rest of the way to the shoe repair shop; after the necessary formalities he enters the office)

SPECIAL COUNSEL: MAJOR ROSS is already here.

MAJOR ROSS: I trust no one followed you?

SENATOR: That's not even funny.

MAJOR ROSS: Never can be too careful.

(MAJOR ROSS is sitting in one of the chairs adjacent to the sofa, smoking a cigarette. He is a nasty piece of work with piercing eyes, a moustache, light colored suit and vest, dark tie and a walking stick, which leans against the sofa)

GEEK (entering from the bathroom): I've checked everywhere for bugs and the rooms are clean.

(The GEEK is a young man with unruly hair and a bad habit of picking his nose. He is a dedicated computer hacker and surveillance expert)

MAJOR ROSS: Can't trust the FBI or the CIA.

GEEK: Absolutely not.

(They all gather round the large conference table, MAJOR ROSS with his back to the wall in front of the only ashtray. The door opens and the last member of the group enters— the MAGICIAN, so named for his ability to make things disappear, such as evidence and on occasion persons)

SPECIAL COUNSEL: Gentlemen—shall we get started? At the last meeting we decided that although there have been damaging leaks to the President's reputation during his first year in office, so far there is no proof as to collusion with Russia by either the President or his campaign staff. We need to dig deeper.

SENATOR: You mean it's time to use the *DOJ Black Book*.

SPECIAL COUNSEL: That's one way to put it.

(The *DOJ Black Book* is a manual of dirty tricks, threats and intimidation procedures to coerce witnesses into testifying against higher-ups, either with real or false evidence or testimony. "Win at all costs" is the prosecutor's goal—no exceptions for Presidents). The *DOJ Black Book* is passed down from one generation to the next and is not in writing. The book's custody, so to speak is presently in the hands of the SENATOR, a member of the Senate Judiciary Committee for several decades)

MAJOR ROSS: I wish to report.

SPECIAL COUNSEL: Please do.

MAJOR ROSS: I have made contact with one of the gardeners who work on the White House lawns and the Rose Garden. He has been watching out for suspicious materials that may indicate a tie to the Russians. Every evening he goes over the grounds with a pooper scooper and normally only picks up dog shit, but last night he found cigarette butts—Russian ones.

(MAJOR ROSS unfolds a small package which reveals three cigarette butts—definitely a Russian brand)

SENATOR: That doesn't prove anything significant. Everyone knows that the Russian Foreign Minister visited the White House recently.

MAJOR ROSS: Nevertheless I expect to be reimbursed for my expenses—a bribe of $100.

MAGICIAN: Watch this.

(The MAGICIAL takes the three cigarette butts and wraps them in a silk handkerchief, shakes it into the air and the three butts are gone)

SPECIAL COUNSEL: We need to find someone to squeeze.

GEEK: Why don't I put a bug in the kitchen at the White House?

SPECIAL COUNSEL: We need someone higher up— much higher.

GEEK: Fine, but we still might learn something interesting while you're still looking for someone to turn into a cooperating witness.

SENATOR: Proceed, but don't get caught.

***

(MAJOR ROSS drives a vegetable truck, accompanied by the GEEK, to the rear entrance of the White House after being admitted with fake documents of the finest quality. MAJOR ROSS, wearing a brown newsboy cap, is minus his vest and walking stick so as to look more like a truck driver. They carry several boxes of vegetables inside and while the GEEK helps the cook's assistant put them away MAJOR ROSS looks around. He picks up a cookbook and leafs through the pages until finding a suspicious looking paper at the back, which finds its way into his pocket)

GEEK (to cook's assistant): The regular driver will be back next week. He bumped his head and got a severe headache all of a sudden.

(He does not mention that the severe headache was caused by a blow to the regular driver's head by MAJOR ROSS, who was quite good at it without killing anyone, unless that was what was desired. MAJOR ROSS drives back to the alley where they had deposited the driver. The GEEK helps put the driver back in the truck after removing his wallet to make it look like a robbery)

MAJOR ROSS: Where did you put the transmitter?

GEEK: With the onions—inside the wooden box on the bottom. They probably won't use up the onions that soon, and then they will just throw away the box. I located the box where it should pick up most of the sounds in the kitchen. Did you find anything interesting in the kitchen?

MAJOR ROSS: Possibly.

GEEK: I've got to go set up the monitoring device and record what goes on in the kitchen.

(MAJOR ROSS and the GEEK go their separate ways. The GEEK monitors the White House kitchen for several days)

***

SENATOR: Let's get down to business.

SPECIAL COUNSEL: Yes. This investigation is moving too slowly. I'm supposed to have an outline of my book about this investigation to my publisher in sixty days.

SENATOR: Any progress to report?

MAJOR ROSS: I believe so. While the GEEK was helping to put away the vegetables I searched the kitchen and found something suspicious—very suspicious.

SPECIAL COUNSEL: Well, spit it out man.

(MAJOR ROSS pulls a sheet of paper from his inside jacket pocket, unfolds it and places it on the table)

SPECIAL COUNSEL: Where did you find that?

MAJOR ROSS: Hidden in the back of a cookbook.

SENATOR: It's printed in Cyrillic. I know that much, but that's it.

SPECIAL COUNSEL: We'll need it translated.

SENATOR: By someone we can trust to keep it secret.

SPECIAL COUNSEL: Obviously.

MAGICIAN: I know someone.

SENATOR: Someone you trust implicitly?

MAGICIAN: Absolutely.

SPECIAL COUNSEL: Who is it?

MAGICIAN: Me.

SPECIAL COUNSEL: You know Russian?

MAGICIAN: No, but I can translate it with computer software.

(The MAGICIAN scans the document into his computer, translates it and borrows a portable printer from the GEEK to print copies)

SPECIAL COUNSEL: It seems to be a list of cooking ingredients.

MAJOR ROSS: It may look like a list of ingredients to you but it is probably a coded message.

SENATOR: Looks to me like a recipe for borscht.

MAJOR ROSS: Borscht is probably the code name for their contact.

SENATOR: It lists beef, potatoes, carrots, beets, cabbage, onions, garlic, dill and sour cream.

MAJOR ROSS: I still think it's a cleverly coded message.

SPECIAL COUNSEL (to GEEK): How is the wiretap going?

GEEK: Fine. I have several hours of recordings.

SENATOR: Anything interesting?

GEEK: Yes. I made a copy of one conversation and can play it for you right now. It's rather incriminating.

(The GEEK plays a short conversation in which a familiar voice states that one of the President's staff met with a Russian official concerning the U.S. election)

SPECIAL COUNSEL: Did you edit that conversation?

GEEK: Yes—just a bit.

SPECIAL COUNSEL: You idiot. That's me speaking during an interview on TV, but that's not what I said. You cut out some of the words.

SENATOR: I thought the voice was familiar.

MAJOR ROSS (to SPECIAL COUNSEL): You need to have someone break that code.

SPECIAL COUNSEL: Yes—I know a former spook we can trust. He's well qualified.

***

(A stranger rings the bell of the shoe repair shop, enters and gives the PROPRIETOR the secret handshake. He hands a package to the PROPRIETOR)

PROPRIETOR: Don't you want to deliver it in person?

(The stranger says no and leaves in a hurry. The PROPRIETOR takes the package upstairs and places it on the conference table. There is a small envelope taped to the top of the package. They all stare at the package until the PROPRIETOR leaves)

SPECIAL COUNSEL: It's from my code-breaker contact. I can tell from the symbol on the top.

SENATOR: Aren't you going to open it?

SPECIAL COUNSEL: Why don't you do the honors?

(The SPECIAL COUNSEL opens the envelope while the SENATOR opens the package to find a plastic container filled with a red liquid and five plastic spoons)

SENATOR: Is this a joke?

SPECIAL COUNSEL: No. It's borscht.

(The SPECIAL COUNSEL holds up the note, which says the paper in question is merely a recipe for borscht, not a code)

GEEK: We might as well try it. I'm hungry.

(The GEEK hands a plastic spoon to MAJOR ROSS, who slaps it out of the GEEK's hands. The GEEK opens the container and offers it to the others who all refuse. He then eats the whole thing)

SPECIAL COUNSEL: We need to start looking more carefully into the background of the President's campaign staff and their activities during the campaign. See what you can find, but in the meantime I will turn my investigators loose.

***

(There is excitement in the air at the next clandestine meeting on Wisconsin Avenue)

MAGICIAN: I think we now have a lever to turn one of the campaign staff, a higher-up who was present at one or more meetings with Russians.

SENATOR: Excellent. Please share the details.

MAGICIAN: The first item is that a senior staffer took a ballot selfie in Maryland, which is one of the states that make it illegal.

SPECIAL COUNSEL: That's not good enough. It's a violation of a state law and not a felony.

SENATOR (to MAGICIAN): I believe you said that you had more.

MAGICIAN: We found a violation of a federal statute – Section 1821 of Title 18 (Crimes and Criminal Procedure).

SENATOR: Never heard of it.

MAGICIAN: Transportation of dentures across a state line by a person not licensed to practice dentistry.

SPECIAL COUNSEL: I don't know if that law has ever been enforced. It's over 70 years old.

MAJOR ROSS: Doesn't matter.

SENATOR: How are you going to prove criminal intent to violate an obscure law that no one's ever heard of?

SPECIAL COUNSEL: The common law requirement of showing criminal intent is no longer necessary as prosecutors are usually able to ignore it and impose a strict liability standard, absent a specific statutory requirement to show criminal intent, and the courts have increasingly gone along with this.

SENATOR: I think I know who it is if he's old enough to be wearing dentures—always wears a bow tie. Let's just call him APPLE for now, like an apple turnover.

(They all laugh at this little joke and after having had their spot of amusement for the day return to business)

SPECIAL COUNSEL: It would be hard to prosecute him if he were wearing his own dentures while crossing the state line.

MAGICIAN: No one was wearing the dentures and APPLE wasn't the one transporting them. It was his son, a medical school student who was bringing them from Virginia to an uncle who lives in Maryland.

MAJOR ROSS: Even easier to turn APPLE if we threaten to prosecute his son and put him in prison.

SENATOR (to MAGICIAN): Let's call the son APPLE JUNIOR to keep things clear. How did you come across this information?

MAGICIAN: APPLE JUNIOR went through a red light soon after he entered Maryland and was stopped by a traffic cop. The cop noticed a package on the front seat of the car, which turned out to contain the dentures. Next to it was a paper bag with some white substance spilling out of it. The cop felt that he had probable cause to search the car and limited his search to the package and the bag once he became aware of the contents—both harmless. The bag contained a powdered-sugar donut. You know how messy those are. The cop was apparently not aware that transporting dentures across state lines was illegal as it was a federal crime. He just gave APPLE JUNIOR a ticket for running a red light.

SENATOR: It sounds a little weak, but I guess it's all we have right now.

MAGICIAN: There are two more possibilities for criminal indictment.

SENATOR (to MAGICIAN): We may change your name to Santa Claus.

MAGICIAN: After inspecting the donut bag the officer tried to hand it back to APPLE JUNIOR, but was told to keep it as APPLE JUNIOR had already eaten three powdered donuts. The officer joked that he might keep it as evidence.

MAJOR ROSS: Sounds like bribery to me.

SPECIAL COUNSEL: Another stretch, but a few stretches add up.

MAGICIAN: This one may be even stronger. Why did APPLE JUNIOR bring dentures back to Maryland?

SENATOR: It must be because his uncle asked him to.

SPECIAL COUNSEL: That makes it a conspiracy to violate Section 1821—another federal crime.

SENATOR: That makes our case stronger against APPLE JUNIOR as far as threatening to indict him. His father will be more likely to turn under this kind of pressure.

SPECIAL COUNSEL: The public is clamoring for an indictment.

GEEK: Only half of them

SPECIAL COUNSEL: That's enough, and my publisher is also eagerly waiting.

SENATOR: Let's proceed.

MAJOR ROSS: I think I can be most effective to start turning the screws on APPLE. I can describe in detail the indignities his son will endure in prison and the effect that grand jury indictments will have on the kid's future, especially if a SWAT-team style arrest with handcuffs is made during class at his university.

GEEK: I thought that the SWAT-team usually went to someone's home and knocked on the door at 2:00 a.m.

SENATOR: No, 2:00 a.m. was the Gestapo in Nazi Germany. The FBI prefers raids at the crack of dawn.

MAJOR ROSS: Okay, threaten to do it at his home with 29 FBI agents with weapons drawn and 17 Swat vehicles. That should make a lasting impression. Leak it to the press; maybe give one of the TV networks an exclusive.

SPECIAL COUNSEL: Very good, MAJOR ROSS. After you have APPLE intimidated I can step in and offer his son immunity from prosecution if he is willing to testify against the President or his family. Depending on what information APPLE can provide I will also offer him a deal, but I need specific facts.

MAGICIAN (to SPECIAL COUNSEL): If you did actually carry out a raid it should help your book sales, especially if you included a DVD of the raid.

GEEK: You got copyright problems if you use film of the raid shot by a TV network, unless you get a license.

SENATOR (to GEEK): It's not a good idea, and they are unlikely to grant a license. Maybe you could go on the raid and shoot a video for the SPECIAL COUNSEL.

GEEK: No way. At the crack of dawn I'm sleeping like a log. I usually don't go to bed before two or three in the morning.

SPECIAL COUNSEL: Let's not think about an actual raid for the time being.

MAJOR ROSS: I could also threaten to shoot APPLE's dog if he has one and he doesn't succumb to pressure on his son. We don't know if they are on good terms. He may think his son is a worthless little shit.

SENATOR: Too risky. If it ever got out we would have PETA and their lawyers after us.

GEEK: What's PETA?

SENATOR: People for the Ethical Treatment of Animals. My wife would probably divorce me—it would be very expensive.

SPECIAL COUNSEL: Killing a dog—man's best friend—would not help my book sales. Hopefully APPLE will cooperate and be able to provide us with incriminating evidence.

SENATOR: You know how a cooperating witness seeking a deal or reduced sentence for himself will often say whatever the prosecutor wants to hear instead of just sticking to the facts.

SPECIAL COUNSEL: I didn't hear that.

<u>THE END</u>

ENOUGH ABOUT MONKEY SELFIES

I want my royalties!

Preface

The bruhaha all started when Wikimedia Commons refused to take down a selfie taken by an Indonesian monkey, actually a macaque. British wildlife photographer David Slater claimed that he owned the copyright to the photograph as his camera had been used. However, it appears that the macaque somehow got hold of the camera and took a now famous self-portrait ("selfie") baring his two large front teeth. Wikimedia refused Slater's take-down request and claims that no one owns the copyright so that the photo is in the public domain. The US Copyright Office agrees and has updated its rules to say that it will not register a copyright for photos taken by animals. *Compendium of U. S. Copyright Office Practices, Third Edition* (2014), hereafter referred to as the *Compendium*. If you think this article is long, try reading all 1,288 pages of the *Compendium*. Subsequent to the filing of the lawsuit mentioned below (*Naruto v. Slater*), Slater asserted that the "monkey" in the selfie is not Naruto, but a female named Ella. However, this article will refer to the celebrity in question as Naruto.

This of course led to numerous articles by lawyers and others about the applicability of copyright laws (primarily those of the United States, with some mention of the United Kingdom, Australia and even the UAE) to photographs taken by monkeys and other animals. The Author decided to write an article much more comprehensive than those scattered about the internet, including coverage of Indonesian and United Kingdom copyright laws. Considering the topic—a frivolous lawsuit filed on behalf of a monkey on the other side of the world—it became obvious that the article though heavy on copyright law should be in the form of satire. After an update on the lawsuit, this is followed by two related satires: BREAKING NEWS: MONKEY'S PETITION BEFORE 9th Circuit Court of Appeals [Unreported Case] and SOLICITOR GENERAL IN A COW PASTURE

Monkey Selfie Copyright Satire

Not to be left out of the commotion, PETA (People for the Ethical Treatment of Animals) added its two-bits by filing a lawsuit against the British photographer (David Slater), his UK company (Wildlife Personalities Limited) and his US publisher (Blurb, Inc.) for damages on behalf of the monkey (dubbed 'Naruto'), claiming that Naruto owns the copyright to the selfie. The suit was filed on behalf of Naruto by PETA and Dr. Antje Engelhardt (a German primatologist who has studied Sula crested macaques for several years) as Next Friends. A cynic might speculate that PETA filed such a frivolous lawsuit to gain publicity, but in this particular case, the Ninth Circuit is certainly the place to be. PETA also asked for a court order allowing it to administer all proceeds from the photos for the benefit of Naruto, his family and his community, including preservation of their habitat. Any such administrator would have to act in a fiduciary capacity on behalf of the copyright owner—Naruto; any funds spent for family or others in the community would appear to be a breach of fiduciary duty. This aspect has apparently been overlooked by PETA and its lawyers.

JURY TRIAL - WITH OR WITHOUT MONKEYS

The complaint also asked for a jury trial. If Defendant files a countersuit, Naruto could ask for a jury of his peers, which he might argue should require macaques (or at least monkeys) on the jury. Undoubtedly, someone would step forward to provide translation services, another opportunity for PETA to do more good works. Although this right is generally restricted to criminal trials, it would be criminal not to apply it here, especially in the Ninth Circuit, where strange things often happen; also, the seventh Amendment of the US Constitution guarantees the right to a jury trial in certain civil cases. Courts have interpreted this to mean a right to an impartial jury chosen from a cross-section or broad spectrum of the community. Application of this rule means that jury selection must be non-discriminatory and cannot exclude a group of which the defendant is a member (monkeys in this case). On the other hand, a defendant is not entitled to have a member of his or her class on the jury. Thus, Naruto could not insist that a jury include a monkey.

How could anyone consider this to be frivolous litigation when the good people at PETA are willing to take on the arduous task of managing Naruto's money on his behalf (and others); not an easy burden in these days of meagre returns at best and gyrations in the securities and commodities markets. In support of PETA, if you look into the large orange-red eyes of Naruto in the selfie, although he is grinning, he is clearly saying "I want my royalties."

<u>IMAGE RIGHTS (WAILIWICK of GUERNSEY)</u>
<u>ORDINANCE</u>

This photo has "personality" written all over it, so one might suggest registration of Naruto's image under The Image Rights (bailiwick of Guernsey) Ordinance (2012). Although few would deny that Naruto has personality, he does not meet the definition of a personage (i.e., a natural person, defined as a human being; a legal person; or a fictional character of a human or non-human) stated in Section 1 of the Ordinance. However, this obstacle was overcome by using Slaters' company instead. On October 31, 2014 the name "Wildlife Personalities Limited" was filed as a 'registered personality', together with the registration of three images. One is the representative photograph of the registered personality, which gives the appearance of being a rectangular shaped logo, containing a photo of Naruto (unnamed) with the words "Wildlife Personalities." The other two images consist of the same photo of Naruto as in the logo and one of another macaque, both unnamed in the filings.

Registration protects the commercial use of personalities and images and extends to unregistered images associated with a registered personality, so that it would cover additional macaque photos "owned" by Wildlife Personalities. The Ordinance protects against unauthorized use of protected images for commercial or financial purposes and has several exceptions, including fair dealing for the purposes of news reporting, commentary and satire. Subject to the foregoing exceptions the image of Naruto is protected under the Guernsey Ordinance, but it remains to be seen to what extent the provisions of this unique law will be enforceable outside of Guernsey.

<u>WHAT LAW APPLIES?</u>

Getting back to the case at hand, the first question should be what law applies—substantive and procedural—as the parties span the globe. PETA, a Virginia corporation, together with Dr. Antje Engelhardt, filed suit in a US District Court in California on behalf of a monkey last known to be living in Indonesia, for copyright violation of selfies taken by the monkey in Indonesia, against British photographer David Slater and his publisher Blurb, Inc. (a Delaware corporation with its principal place of business in San Francisco), and thrown in for good measure (as lawyers tend to do) a UK limited company (Wildlife Personalities, Ltd) owned by Slater, with no apparent US contacts. Why wasn't Wikimedia Commons also listed as a defendant? What we have here is a bowl of animal crackers with elements of the Marx Brothers.

Naruto's "Complaint for Copyright Infringement" alleges that Naruto made the monkey selfies in Sulawesi, Indonesia, that none of these images is a "United States Work," and therefore no US copyright registration is required to maintain the action. The case should have been tossed out right there for failing to plead sufficiently, as the crucial point is where the selfie was first published, not where it was made. In order to "not be a United States Work" the plaintiff is required to plead that the selfie was first "published" (not made) outside the United States, which as it turns out was the United Kingdom. "Once the plaintiff has proven publication, he must then prove that the publication was, in fact, the first publication, and that the geographic extent of his first publication diverges from the statutory definition of a 'United States Work.'" *Kernel Records Oy v. Mosley* 934 F.3d 1294 (11th Cir. 2012). You might think this would prompt someone to consider which copyright law should apply, but apparently not; very few of the "monkey selfie" articles mention the question of jurisdiction or applicable law in any detail, if at all.

Defendants filed a motion to dismiss the complaint on the basis of lack of standing and failure to state a claim upon which relief can be granted, but did not request dismissal on the grounds of *forum non conveniens*, the proper forum being Indonesia on the basis that its copyright law should apply rather than US copyright law. *Halo Creative & Design Ltd. v. Comptoir Des Indes, Inc.*, 816 F.3d 1366 (Fed. Cir., 2016). Aside from creativity or originality requirements, copyright comes into existence immediately upon an author taking a picture with a camera as it then becomes fixed in a tangible medium—the photo having been taken in Indonesia. Defendants' motion also failed to request dismissal based on lack of personal jurisdiction—discussed below.

SPIDERMAN's NINTH CIRCUIT LONG-ARM JURISDICTIONAL REACH

The District Court in *Naruto v. Slater* did not need Spiderman to stretch its long-arm jurisdiction from San Francisco to London (and then backtrack to Wales). It is not well-known, but federal and state judges in the Ninth Circuit not only have law clerks, but have ready access to chiropractors to alleviate the symptoms caused by frequent long-arm stretching.

The plaintiffs alleged that the District Court had subject matter jurisdiction pursuant to 28 U.S.C. §§ 1331 and 1338(a) based on the suit arising under US copyright law, not mentioning an alternative basis for jurisdiction based on diversity of citizenship under § 1332, which might have made some interesting commentary and would have required a finding that Naruto was a citizen or subject of a foreign state (Indonesia), keeping in mind that the plaintiff was Naruto, not PETA or Dr. Engelhardt (merely Next Friends).

There is no federal statute governing personal jurisdiction concerning copyright law, hence the law of the state in which the district court sits—California—applies. *Kip Rano v. Sipa Press, Inc.* 987 F.2d 580 (9th Cir. 1993), which also states that litigation against an alien defendant requires a higher jurisdictional barrier than litigation against a citizen of a sister state. California has adopted a typical long-arm statute, rendering jurisdiction coextensive with the outer limits of due process. *Data Disc v. System Tech Assoc.*, 557 F.2d 1280 (9th Cir. 1977). The District Court apparently accepted Plaintiffs' assertion (without discussion) that it had personal jurisdiction over Slater and Wildlife Personalities Limited (a UK company) based on allegations that a substantial part of their infringing conduct occurred in its judicial district. Personal jurisdiction over Blurb, Inc. was based on the location of its principal place of business and its alleged copyright infringement occurring in the judicial district.

On a motion to dismiss, all factual allegations set forth in the complaint are taken as true and construed in the light most favorable to the plaintiff. *Lee v. City of Los Angeles*, 250 F.3d 668 (9th Cir. 2008). Although the District Court in *Naruto v. Slater* stated that the "court is not required to accept as true 'allegations that are merely conclusory, unwarranted deductions of fact, or unreasonable inferences,'" it seems to have ignored such conclusory allegations, namely that a "substantial" part of the infringing conduct occurred in California—as discussed next.

PERSONAL JURISDICTION SPANS THE GLOBE

The assertion of personal jurisdiction over David Slater (a resident of the United Kingdom) based on an allegation that a "substantial part" of his infringing conduct occurred 'in this judicial district' (Northern California) is unsupported by any factual allegations. Slater is an internationally known wildlife photographer located in the United Kingdom who sells images—not books—online from his UK website (www.djsphotography.co.uk) to customers around the world; the statement that a substantial part of his infringement (selling photos) in Northern California seems quite a stretch, but maybe not in the Ninth Circuit. Sales of these images occur in the UK either upon electronic transmission—not upon delivery in California or elsewhere—or upon shipment of prints from the UK. Jurisdiction over Slater insofar as relying on the infringement occurring in California is also questionable in light of the recent decision in *Pablo Star Ltd. v. The Welsh Government* (S.D.N.Y. Mar. 16. 2016).

The book distribution agreement between Blurb and Slater grants Blurb a non-exclusive license to reproduce, display, modify and reformat the content of a book—"Wildlife Personalities"—that contains photos of Naruto for purposes of printing, distribution and making it available through the Blurb Bookstore. Customers who buy the book through the Bookstore are deemed to be Blurb's customers, not Slater's. Although Blurb's principal place of business is in California, it—not Slater—sells books online to purchasers, some of whom may be in California. He is not engaging in any infringing activity by selling books in California; Slater is receiving royalties from an independent contractor under a mere licensing agreement which is non-exclusive. However, even the existence of an exclusive license agreement does not establish minimum contacts for purposes of personal jurisdiction without additional terms and conditions beyond the payment of royalties, such as granting both parties the right to litigate infringement cases or granting the licensor the right to exercise control over the licensee's sales or marketing activities. *Breckenridge Pharm., Inc. v. Metabolite Labs, Inc.,* 444 F. 3d 1356 (2006). Blurb is not Slater's agent as he exercises no control over Blurb or its marketing policies; therefore its activities in California should not be imputed to Slater for jurisdictional purposes. *Armstrong v. Virgin Records, Ltd.,* 91 F. Supp. 2d 628 (2000).

DID EVERYONE FORGET ABOUT INDONESIAN COPYRIGHT LAW?

The District Court in effect accepted jurisdiction and granted the motion to dismiss so let us move on to substantive law, which is more important to this discussion. First, let us dispose of Indonesian copyright law. Paragraph 2 of Article 1 states: "Author shall mean a person or several persons jointly upon whose inspiration a Work is produced, based on the intellectual ability, imagination, dexterity, skill or expertise manifested in a distinct form and is of a personal nature." The Indonesian Copyright Act does not define "person," but to start with it cannot include a legal entity in view of the wording of Paragraph 11, which defines a Producer of a Phonogram as a person or legal corporate body. Paragraph 14, which uses the words "his/her works" in reference to the rights obtained from a "Copyright Holder" by a licensee, supports the interpretation that the term "person" should be restricted to "individuals." Stronger support is found in Paragraph 3 of Article 10, which refers to "any person who is not a citizen of Indonesia," with respect to permission concerning certain Works owned by the Indonesian Government.

Sorry, Naruto, but it looks like your homeland will not treat you as an author.

UK COPYRIGHT LAW

Next, let us consider UK copyright law, which provided under the 1956 Copyright Act that the author of a photograph was the person who at the time the photograph was taken "owned the material on which it was taken" but unfortunately for Slater this is no longer UK law.

The Copyright, Designs and Patents Act 1988 (the "CDPA") states in section 9 (1): In this Part "author," in relation to a work, means the person who creates it. "Person" is not defined, but common definitions in a business or legal context generally include an individual, body corporate, partnership, etc. The last support for the position that animals may not be authors (and thus not copyright owners) under UK copyright law is found in Section 154 (1), which provides copyright protection for qualified authors (e.g., a British citizen, an individual domiciled or resident in the UK, or a body corporate, etc.).

Fact sheet P-01: UK Copyright Law of the UK Copyright Service states that "To qualify, a work should be regarded as original, and exhibit a degree of labor, skill or judgment." Unlike US copyright law, creativity is not required for originality in under UK copyright law. The IPO has indicated that under UK law animals cannot own copyrights, but left open the ownership question as to the photographer in the case of animal selfies.

IS NARUTO's SELFIE A COMPUTER GENERATED WORK UNDER UK COPYRIGHT LAW?

It has been suggested that a photographer may be able to claim UK copyright of animal selfies based on computer-generated art (depending on the circumstances), which would require the use of a digital camera rather than an old-fashioned camera with a roll of film. Before considering this possibility we must first review the rules governing the copyright of photographs under UK copyright law.

Copyright exists for original artistic works under the CDPA, which in section 4 (1) (a) defines "artistic work" as "a graphic work, photograph, sculpture or collage irrespective of artistic quality." CDPA section 4 (2) states: "Photograph" means a 'recording of light or other radiation on any medium on which an image is produced or from which an image may by any means be produced, and which is not part of a film.'"

Section 9 (3) of the CDPA states: In the case of literary, dramatic, musical or artistic work which is computer generated, the author shall be taken to be the person by whom the arrangements necessary for the creation of the work are undertaken. Section 178 defines computer-generated work as work generated by a computer in circumstances such that there is no human author of it, thus by implication excluding computer-aided work. Although Sections 9 (3) and 178 of the CDPA refer to "computer-generated" works, it is the software, not the computer, which creates the works. Thus, undue emphasis should not be placed on the word "computer." Digital cameras, like printers and scanners, are in effect special-purpose computers, which have internally stored firmware, similar to software in a computer. It should not be that difficult to justify pictures taken by a digital camera as being computer-generated, with the author (under UK law) being the person who makes the arrangements necessary for the creation of the work. This might possibly be helpful to

Slater, depending on his involvement—which may not be enough in this case.

WATCH OUT WHAT YOU ASK FOR

Before we leave the topic of photographs taken by digital cameras qualifying for copyright protection as computer-generated work, it is important to note that the copyright period is only 50 years, compared to the life of the author plus 70 years for work qualifying as a "photograph" under CDPA section 4 (2). This difference might cause classification problems in some situations, depending on the circumstances under which the work was created, as to whether a particular work would be entitled to protection for the life of the author plus 70 years or only 50 years.

US COPYRIGHT LAW

The discussion must necessarily move on to US copyright law, which is the focus of *Naruto v. Slater* and the endless flow of articles that has resulted. In order for a work to be protected under US copyright law, it must be an original creation of an author and be fixed in a tangible medium of expression (such as a computer file or written on a piece of paper, for which a paper napkin in a bar or restaurant will do). Not much is required as far as originality is concerned, which means merely that the material is original as to the author and has not been copied from someone else's work. Creativity (even if mediocre and lacking in quality) is sometimes also mentioned as a requirement in the US, as well as some intellectual endeavor, which is where animals seem to fail the requirements of being authors.

In *Hein v. Harris* 175 F. 875 (C.C.S.D.N.Y. 1910), aff'd 183 Fed. 107 (2d Cir. 1923), a copyright infringement case in which *Arab Love Song* was compared to *I Think I Hear a*

Woodpecker, Judge Learned Hand stated: "The lack of originality and musical merit in both songs is of no consequence. While the public taste continues to give pecuniary value to a composition of no artistic excellence, the court must continue to recognize the value so created."

A BRIEF COMMENT ON PETA's APPEAL

In its appeal to the Ninth Circuit, Plaintiffs complain that the District Court departed from the well-established norm that every photograph is entitled to copyright protection, citing *Ets-Hokin v. Skyy Spirits, Inc*, 225 F.3d 1068 (9th Cir. 2000), and that all photographs are sufficiently original by their nature to merit copyright protection. *Los Angeles News Service v. Tullo,* 973 F.2d 791 (9th Cir. 1992). The focus of these statements is whether photographs meet the low threshold of originality for copyright protection. These statements, standing alone are not the law. For copyright protection, a photograph must have an author. Upon climbing to the top of a steep rocky mountain, a hiker needing to catch his or her breath may remove a backpack and place a camera on the ground or upon a rock. If a gust of wind sweeps up the camera and it bounces down the mountainside, snapping pictures each time its button hits a rock at just the right angle, the resulting photographs may be original but will have no author and therefore no copyright protection, although someone—not mentioning any names—might come forward and claim the wind as the author.

WHO OR WHAT IS AN AUTHOR?

The term "author" is not defined in the US copyright statute, but the opinion of the US Copyright Office is that an author must be a human, as discussed further below. Under UK copyright law the "author" is the "person" who creates the work, subject to special rules for motion pictures, sound recordings, etc. Although "person" is not defined in the UK statute either, the ordinary meaning of persons in a business or legal context often includes individuals, corporations and other entities, but not animals. Under both US and UK law, any work that does not have an author is considered by default to be in the public domain.

THE ALMIGHTY COMPENDIUM OF THE US COPYRIGHT OFFICE

NOTE: The following has not been verified and might be fake news.

> Is was a sunny spring day in Washington, DC, not a cloud in the sky, a good day for outdoor picnics, when suddenly the sky turned black, accompanied by thunder and lightning. Then, just as quickly, the sky began to clear over the building on Independence Avenue that houses the U.S. Copyright Office, first with an opening in the middle of the sky. Through it a noisy helicopter descended and out stepped a tall bearded man wearing long flowing robes and sandals, bearing a striking resemblance to the deceased actor Charlton Heston. The helicopter rotors became silent and the few employees who were enjoying a lunch break on the lawn rushed over to see what was happening. The tall bearded man held up a thick book and spoke in a commanding voice:

> Behold, I am the prophet Moses and I bring you the word of God. Those who are employed by the copyright office step forward and listen carefully. There is far too much chaos and confusion in the

area of copyright law, which benefits only the lawyers, not God's intention, and causes much stress to others. I bring you a *Compendium* of copyright rules and regulations with a clear interpretation of the law. God thought that the *Ten Commandments* were quite clear, but possibly not because of their brevity. Since mankind has generally ignored the *Ten Commandments*, the *Compendium* contains a total of 1,288 pages to avoid any possible misunderstandings. When you quote the *Compendium* to lawyers and judges you must make it clear that this is the word of God, and must be strictly construed.

The US Copyright Office sets forth several general rules in Chapter 300 of its *Compendium* regarding copyrightable authorship and what can be registered, or more accurately, what it is willing to register. Sec. 306 states an overall rule that the US Copyright Office will register an original work of authorship only if created by a human being. It also states that copyright law only protects "the fruits of intellectual labor" that "are founded in the creative powers of the mind," citing *Trade-Mark Cases*, 111 U.S. 53, 58 (1884). Sec. 313.2 states that the "Office will not register works produced by nature, animals or plants," including (under the examples) a photograph taken by a monkey or a mural painted by an elephant. This article will return to elephant paintings later. Notwithstanding these pronouncements, this does not mean that a photograph taken by an animal may not be copyrighted by a human being under any circumstances whatsoever; see further discussion below, citing *Compendium* Sec. 802.5(C).

In discussing visual arts, which include photographs and paintings, Sec. 906 states that works not created by a human being are not eligible for copyright protection, a refrain inserted repeatedly throughout the *Compendium*. Perhaps the US Copyright Office believes in the old adage that if you repeat something enough times everyone will believe it without question. The *Compendium* is not a law; it contains the rules for registering copyrights, based on the interpretation of the copyright statute by the US copyright Office and court cases cited in the *Compendium*. Although the courts give deference to the regulations and opinions of the US Copyright office, the question is still before the courts as PETA has appealed its case to the Ninth Circuit, and may not stop there.

US COPYRIGHT OFFICE RATES CHIMPANZEE VIDEOS LOWER THAN 'B' MOVIES

Sec. 807(C) states that a motion picture must contain creative human authorship, and that a chimpanzee is not an author where it picks up a video camera, inadvertently turns it on and records images. Note the word "inadvertently." Chimpanzee videos (where a chimpanzee is directed to use a video camera instead of picking it up inadvertently) might be copyrighted by someone other than the animal, such as a human who participated sufficiently in the work's creation so as to qualify as its author, provided that the work meets the originality and creative requirements for copyright.

JOINT AUTHORS?

Assuming for argument that Naruto is the author of his selfies could Slater be considered as a joint author? A joint work is one created by two or more co-authors with the intention that their contributions be merged into inseparable parts of a unitary whole (US) or that the contribution of each author is not distinct (UK). Each one must contribute copyrightable subject matter to the work; one who merely contributes ideas is not a joint author. The selfie cannot be considered as a joint work, making the photographer a co-author, because Slater, unlike Naruto, participated in none of the actions that resulted in the taking of the selfie. In addition, there was no intention between them to be co-authors.

PAINTINGS OF HARD WORKING CHIMPANZEE, HORSE and ELEPHANT DUMPED INTO PUBLIC DOMAIN

In contrast to selfies, there are numerous examples of paintings created by animals: Congo, a chimpanzee; Kissu, the horse; and Ruby, the elephant. These may involve more effort than merely swishing a brush at a canvas, but the results are generally considered to be in the public domain. The owner of such an animal might be able to claim authorship if he or she sufficiently directed the actions of the animal in creating a painting. For example, the creative input of the animal's owner might include selecting the colors of paint, changing the position of a canvas during the creation of the painting, and directing the animal to start, stop and resume painting until the owner deems the project finished. On the other hand, disregarding the "human being" requirement, an elephant may be able to provide creative input in some cases. An example might be where six buckets of paint are set out near a canvas, each a different color, with a separate brush in each bucket; without human prompting the elephant might pick up a brush from a bucket of its choosing, paint for a while and then try another color until it decided to stop painting. It might even choose not to use all of the colors. If PETA's theory is correct, the elephant in such cases would be an author and own the copyright. Contrast that scenario with some of the animals in elephant centers in Indonesia, where elephant creativity appears to be lacking as they paint the same picture over and over (suggesting training). Similar to leading a witness in a trial, the mahouts (trainers) apparently tug the ear of the elephant up, down or sideways, resulting in the elephant moving the paintbrush in a corresponding direction on the canvas.

COPYRIGHT BY USING LOAN-OUT COMPANIES HIRED TO PROVIDE ANIMALS TO PAINT

There is another possible way for a person to claim authorship of artwork created by animals—the "work-made-for-hire" doctrine. The "author" is the owner of the copyright, unless it involves work-made-for-hire. A "work-made-for-hire" is (1) a work made by an employee for his or her employer, or (2) a work (limited to nine specific categories, including contributions to a collective work, supplemental work or compilation) made by an independent contractor if the parties expressly agree in a written instrument signed in advance that the work shall be considered as a "work-made-for-hire."

An animal cannot be an employee, even if owned by an individual, and is excluded by the use of the words 'his or her employer' in clause (1). That leaves the independent contractor route under clause (2), the wording of which is not specifically restricted to individuals. On the other hand, Sec. 802.5(C) of the Compendium states: "To be copyrightable, musical works, like all works of authorship, must be of human origin." However, compare *Urania Foundation v. Maaherra*, 114 F.3d 955 (1997) in which the Ninth Circuit Court of Appeals stated that the copyright laws do not expressly require "human" authorship, but that some element of human creativity must have occurred for a work to be copyrightable. The case involved copyright to a book allegedly authored by celestial beings and transcribed by mere mortals, a most appropriate case for the Ninth Circuit.

Actors often form wholly owned corporations (or limited liability companies) which act as loan-out companies to contract out their services to motion picture production companies. The loan-out company acts as an independent contractor in providing services to the production company, usually those of its sole owner. A client (individual or legal entity) could be deemed to be the author of a painting under a work-for-hire contract with a loan-out company which used one of its employees to create the painting if the work fell within one of the nine work-for-hire categories.

There is no rule which states that the services provided by a loan-out company must be provided by its own 'employees', although such an assumption might be made from the second example under Sec. 802.8(E) of the *Compendium*, discussed below, where the author is listed as an LLC with respect to musical works created as works made for hire. Art works are not one of the nine categories listed as a work for hire under clause (2); therefore, a painting—by an animal or a human—must fall under one of the nine specified categories to be a work for hire by an independent contractor. The most likely categories would be as a "contribution to a collective work," a "supplementary work," or a "compilation." The use of loan-out companies for musical animals is discussed below.

PROBLEMS LOCATING ANIMALS' HEIRS TO RECLAIM COPYRIGHTS FROM LICENSEES

Assuming that PETA is correct—that animals may be authors and owners of their selfies—there are additional issues which to date have been overlooked and require consideration. Copyright protection varies depending on the type of work and the country. For photographs, the period (in the US) is the life of the author plus 70 years or 95 years from publication for a "work-made-for-hire."

The US Copyright Act allows authors or certain heirs to reclaim their copyrights by terminating publishers' or licensees' rights after 35 years (56 years for pre-1978 works) from the date of a published work, but only if the works are not works-made-for-hire. When a copyright owning animal dies, how do you determine or locate its heirs. Inasmuch as an animal is incapable of executing a will, there will be no executor, so it would be necessary for an administrator to be appointed by a court. Searching for the heirs may require substantial travel at the expense of the estate, which may end up with peanuts. If the heirs are monkeys, who will complain about such results? Such tedious travel around the globe (possibly through forests and mosquito infested jungles) in search of the heirs would no doubt justify the administrator in charging the estate for first-class airfare and hotel accommodations, as well as foot massages.

DON'T FORGET AN AUTHORS' MORAL RIGHTS – A BLACK & WHITE PRINT OF A NARUTO SELFIE IS A NO, NO

Wait! There is one more consideration if an animal is an author: "Droit moral" or "moral rights." These include several types of rights, but the only relevant one is the right to object to derogatory treatment of a copyrighted work (known as the "right of integrity"), which prevents certain changes to the author's work without permission. Thus, the selfies of Naruto (if the author) cannot be altered without his permission in jurisdictions where "droit moral" is in force, which might prohibit publication of his photos in black and white as well as other changes without the author's permission. This brings to mind the unsuccessful 1980's objections from film directors over the colorization of their old black-and-white films; the US Copyright Office ruled that the copyright owner of a black-and-white film had the legal right to colorize it, the colorization being a derivative work with a separate copyright. Naruto would be better protected in France where in 1988 a French court prohibited the premiere TV broadcast of a colorized version of John Huston's *Asphalt Jungle* based on the right of integrity under the French doctrine of droit moral.

In Europe, it is generally not possible for authors to assign or even waive their moral rights, but contracts often require the author to agree not to enforce these rights. There may also be a requirement for the author to "assert" these moral rights before they can be enforced. In the United Kingdom, moral rights may be waived, but not assigned. No doubt, some well-intended group would step forward and be willing to assert, waive or assign an animal's moral rights on its behalf when appropriate—for royalties.

MONKEYS ARE NOT THE ONLY NON-HUMAN AUTHORS

Enough about animals and selfies, especially monkeys who are hogging the limelight. Missing from the endless discussion of monkeys as authors is the possibility that other living things such as trees may be authors. Why not? Just because humans share more DNA with monkeys than with trees is no reason to discriminate against trees and deny them authorship. This area of discussion must necessarily begin with a focus on the copyright of music rather than literary property, photographs or paintings.

FIRST - MUSIC COPYRIGHT FOR ANIMALS

The copyright of music involves more aspects than the copyright of photographs, although the same general principals apply: authorship, originality, fixation, etc. There are two separate categories for music: musical works and sound recordings. Musical works are usually divided into lyrics (words) and melody, each with its own copyright, although a melody may exist without words. There may be more than one author, as where one person writes the lyrics and another the melody or both may be written by the same person. A separate copyright exists in the sound recording, although permission (generally in the form of a mechanical license) must be obtained from the owner or owners of the musical work to record it. The producer of the sound recording is usually treated as the author, although the *Compendium* has more to say about this.

Returning to originality, although only a bare minimum of creativity is necessary, there is a similarity between the requirements for literary and musical works. Ideas may not be copyrighted, only the expression of ideas when fixed in tangible form. Similar to words and short phrases, which are not subject to copyright, mere sounds (such as those of a banjo) or a few musical notes standing alone cannot be copyrighted; only the expression of sounds, as in a musical composition, may be copyrighted. Regarding creative expression, Sec. 803.5 (B) states in part: "Short sound recordings may lack a sufficient amount of authorship to be copyrightable (just as words and short textual phrases are not copyrightable)."

Sound recordings are "works that result from the fixation of a series of musical, spoken, or other sounds, but not including sounds accompanying a motion picture or other audiovisual work, regardless of the nature of the material objects, such as disks, tapes or other phono records, in which they are embodied." 17 U.S.C. § 101. A series of musical, spoken, or other sounds requires a temporal succession of sounds rather than a single sound expressed horizontally or simultaneous sounds expressed vertically, such as in a chord. *Compendium*, Sec. 803.1. This would disqualify certain basic sounds of animals or trees.

THE THAI ELEPHANT ORCHESTRA – MUSICAL COMPOSITIONS

Works that contain only a de minimis amount of original expression, such as a musical phrase of three notes or a sound recording consisting of a single tone, are not copyrightable. *Compendium*, Sec. 313.4(B). This is hardly the case with the Thai Elephant Orchestra in Lampang, Northern Thailand—a group of 14 Asian elephants. The elephants play on large gongs, drums, chimes, and metal and wooden marimba-like instruments, often using mallets of different sizes, and even large harmonicas. Elephants have a sense of rhythm and generally improvise as they play what they want; these seem to have minimal supervision by caretakers or trainers. You can watch a documentary online about the Thai Elephant Orchestra, which includes the performances of several elephants, at [http://www.davesoldier.com/thaiorch.html]. It seems that most people who have heard the elephant orchestra consider their efforts to be music instead of noise, whether or not they like it. Justice Learned Hand (if he were alive) would no doubt reach the opposite conclusion if his opinion in *Hein v. Harris* is anything to go by—describing 'rag-time' as the lowest grade of the musical art.

JOINT AUTHORS OR NOT?

Joint works are works prepared by two or more authors with the intention at the time of creation that their contributions merge into inseparable or interdependent parts of a unitary whole. If the authors did not intend for their separate elements to be merged into an interdependent whole, the separate copyrightable elements should be registered as separate works. *Compendium,* Sec. 801.6. Absent such intent, the elephants cannot qualify as joint authors, but they might qualify as individual authors of their relative contributions—works. *Compendium,* Sec. 309 requires that the work contain at least a minimum amount of creative authorship that is original to the author. In this case, the contribution of each elephant must be tested separately. Some, or maybe none of them, might meet this requirement. However, the number of elephants may make the creative contribution of each one minimal and in any event difficult to measure. It is better to leave it at that and move on to sound recordings. The musical composition of the Thai Elephant Orchestra is a collaborative work, which overall, together with the creative input of the producer, should satisfy the copyright requirements for a sound recording (with the producer being its author).

We will skip music ownership (which may be divided among the composer of the lyrics and/or the melody, sheet music publishers, record labels, and performing rights) and concentrate on authorship. It should be noted that transcribing or fixing a musical work in and of itself does not constitute authorship. *Compendium,* Sec 802.8(B). This statement seems to conflict with the Ninth Circuit's decision in *Urania Foundation v. Maaherra* (discussed above), which involved copyright to a book allegedly authored by celestial beings and transcribed by mere mortals.

MUSICAL COMPOSITIONS AND SOUND RECORDINGS

There may be more than one author for a musical composition or sound recording. However, in the case of a sound recording the producer is usually treated as the author and the record label as the owner. Although it is possible for band members to be joint owners of a sound recording, usually they are under work-for-hire contracts or hired as employees, and are not joint authors. Other possible joint authors include (1) session musicians, who drop in (or are invited) to join a music session; (2) guest musicians, who may be invited up to the stage at a live performance; and (3) soloists who make a distinctive contribution to a performance. In the first two situations, session or guest musicians would have to make an important contribution to the session or performance to become joint authors and/or be entitled to a share of profits. Even absent an intention of the parties to be joint authors, a share of profits still may be the best result that can be obtained. What if an elephant dropped in uninvited to a session of the Thai Elephant Orchestra and contributed a wonderful drum solo—royalties but not authorship?

Non-featured musicians (such as background singers) are not potential joint authors, as they generally do not make substantial creative contributions and the intent to be joint authors is missing; also, they usually work as employees. Under UK copyright law, the author of a sound recording is the producer, but the copyright owner is usually the person (often a record company) who pays for the recording. CDPA Section 9 (2)(aa).

Compendium Section 803.3 states that there are two types of sound recording authorship—performance authorship and production authorship. Either one will require a minimum amount of creative authorship. Generally, both the performer and the producer of a sound recording of a musical performance or spoken word performance contribute copyrightable authorship to the sound recording. In some cases, however, the main or sole contribution may be production authorship (as in a recording of bird songs, where there is no human performance) or the main contribution may be performance authorship (as in a recorded performance where the only production involved is to push the "record" button). Examples of production authorship in a sound recording include capturing and manipulating sounds, and compiling and editing those sounds to make a final recording. On the other hand, an executive producer (limited to the financing and administration of a recording, rather than being creatively involved in the recording) is not an author under US copyright law.

Now that the basic copyright rules for musical compositions and sound recordings have been outlined, their application will be discussed in relation to the creation and authorship of works by animals and then trees. Yes, trees!

ANIMALS & MUSICAL COMPOSITIONS

The *Compendium* states that "to be copyrightable, musical works, like all works of authorship, must be of human origin" and that "A musical work created solely by an animal would not be registerable, such as a bird song or whale song." Sec 802.5(C). Did you read the second statement too quickly and overlook the word solely? Animal songs can be copyrighted by someone other than the animal, such as a human who participated sufficiently in the work's creation so as to qualify as its author, provided the work meets the originality and creative requirements for copyright.

Notwithstanding the foregoing, the "author" need not always be a human as an entity such as a corporation or LLC may be registered as the author of a work under one of the work-made-for-hire exceptions. Because animals cannot be employees, the second exception (discussed above) would have to be availed of—a work made by an independent contractor (using animals to create the musical sounds) if the parties agree in writing (in advance) that the work will be considered as a "work-made-for-hire."

Since musical works are not one of the nine categories listed in the work-made-for-hire definition, a musical work must fall under one of those categories to be considered a work-made-for-hire; the most likely categories would be as a "contribution to a collective work," a "supplementary work," or a "compilation." *Compendium*, Sec 802.8(E). The second example allows an applicant to identify an LLC as the author of music in the case of a work that is made for hire … and states that it appears that the company employs people to compose the music. However, there is no specific requirement in the *Compendium* that an independent contractor use employees or its own independent contractors who are individuals or even humans. See the discussion above concerning possible use of animals by loan-out companies to create paintings. In addition to an individual independent contractor, it would seem that a loan-out company, which own or rent animals, could enter into a contract to provide services as an independent contractor to a person who as a result, would be the author of any music or paintings made by the loaned-out animals. The only obstacle, other than possible complaints from animal rights groups, is that the commissioned work would have to fit into one of the nine categories that constitute works-made-for hire, no problem for a creative lawyer.

TREES & MUSICAL COMPOSITIONS

If PETA is correct that animals may be authors for copyright purposes, why should not other living things— such as trees—also qualify as authors in appropriate situations? Trees (as well as animals) have been protected by various laws (e.g., the Forestry Reserve Act of 1897) over the years, so there is some basis that trees have rights. Supreme Court Justice William O. Douglas, dissenting in *Sierra Club v. Morton*, 405 U.S. 729 (1972), noted that inanimate objects are sometimes parties in litigation and asserted that natural resources, such as trees, ought to have standing to sue for their own protection. It does not make them humans, but trees do share some DNA with humans, although to a lesser extent than animals. Unlike monkeys, trees do not have brains but are capable of movement; they move towards light in response to phototropism. With respect to trees moving, consider Monty Python's *The Walking Tree of Dahomey*, (a sketch with David Attenborough) in which the legendary walking tree of Dahomey—Quercus Nicholas Parsonus—walked over two thousand miles on its way to Cape Town. Proof of this feat is lacking unfortunately as Attenborough informs us that they have just missed the famous walking tree. Let us now turn to copyright law as it applies to trees.

The obvious category for trees is musical compositions. Because trees themselves are incapable of reducing their musical sounds to paper—ironic since paper comes from trees—the sounds can be fixed in permanent form only by capturing them in sound recordings. One might assume that musical compositions are usually first created by writing the lyrics and melody on a piece of paper or in a computer file, followed by a sound recording some time later. However, these steps can occur simultaneously, as where the song writer makes a sound recording the first time he or she performs the musical work (without having previously written it down). In this case, separate copyrights will result simultaneously, one for the musical composition and another for the sound recording. This would be the only method of fixation where a tree is the author, because there is no way to reduce the musical sounds of a tree to a fixed form prior to making a sound recording. The fact that a tree is incapable of independently creating a copyrighted musical composition "prior" to its recording is not relevant to its ultimate copyright; the recording simultaneously creates separate copyrights for the melody and another for the sound recording. There is no requirement that a sound recording be of an existing copyrighted musical composition. For example, in the case of a new recording of music in the public domain, only one work would be copyrighted—the new sound recording, not the underlying musical composition.

Whether the sounds of trees are considered music or merely sounds is not determinative as performance authorship includes "playing an instrument, singing, or speaking, or creating other sounds which are captured and fixed in a sound recording." *Compendium*, Sec. 803.3(A). However, Sec. 802.5(B) states that to be copyrightable, "a musical work must contain a sufficient amount of creative expression." Sec. 313.4(C) states: "short musical phrases consisting of only a few musical notes standing alone are not copyrightable," and gives clock chimes as an example. Clock chimes repeat the same sound each time, whereas members of the Thai Elephant Orchestra (in contrast) produce a series of different musical sounds each time they move their trunks and hit a row of chimes.

Trees make sounds: branches creak or break off; snow or ice may fall off branches; leaves rustle and branches sway in the wind; branches may make a noise returning to position as squirrels jump from one branch to the next; leaves or pine cones may fall to the ground or on a nearby tin roof. A whistling sound may occur as the wind blows through the branches, leaves, or holes in the tree. Although one can argue that some of these actions are the result of the wind, it must be remembered that the tree (unlike the wind) is a living thing and is reacting to the wind. At best, the wind might be a co-author, but cannot manifest its consent in writing so must be disregarded, leaving (no pun intended) the tree as sole author. This avoids the problem of locating the wind under UK copyright law, where all joint owners of copyrighted material must consent to its licensing.

Although most of these sounds may not rise to the level of musical compositions, sound recordings are not limited to music and may consist of other sounds. However, since some degree of creativity (though not artistic merit) is required it is probably best to disregard all tree sounds other than musical ones. Possible musical compositions might consist of a tree dropping its pine cones in a syncopated manner on a metal container resting at its base (similar to a drum solo), or a whistling melody as a tree bends its branches to allow the wind to pass. If this is a stretch of the imagination, such inspiration must have emanated from the Ninth Circuit. Continuing, we can disregard any birds singing in the background, as they are not making a substantial creative contribution to the work, similar to background singers who appear with a lead singer, although in the case of background singers this contingency is usually eliminated by contract.

Speaking or narration might be added to the sound recording to make it more interesting, with the result that the writer or narrator could become a joint author of a tree if the obstacle of joint authorship—intention—could be overcome. However, since there can be no such joint intent, at best they would be individual authors of their relative contributions. If the sounds are not deemed to be musical compositions there would not be a separate copyright, only a copyright for the sound recording of which the producer (not the tree) would be the author.

PETA, for example, could be appointed to collect the royalties for the trees in question, which might be a nice fit as monkeys often live in trees or at least swing from them. On the other hand, a conflict of interest might arise in representing both trees and monkeys. There could also be a conflict of interest for lawyers who provide legal representation for a tree and a human joint author. Lawyers should decide this question for themselves, as referral of the question to their state bar association might produce an unwanted response. Lawyers who want to expand their practice should probably limit representation to animals and not trees.

APPEAL OF NATUTO v. SLATER

The District Court dismissed Naruto's case on January 29, 2016 for lack of standing; however, PETA filed an appeal on behalf of Naruto to the Ninth Circuit on March 20, 2016. The lower court did not rule on Slater's possible copyright ownership, or whether the selfie was in the public domain. They say that location is everything; the Ninth Circuit is the place to be if you are seeking a novel interpretation of copyright law, where going bananas and tossing copyright law on its head is not unheard of, if you remember *Garcia v. Google*, 786 F.3d 733 (9th Cir. 2015), though the Court of Appeals (sitting in en banc) dissolved the three-judge panel's amended takedown injunction against Google.

PETA's odds might be better if the appeal is heard by the right three-judge panel instead of a hearing (en banc) by the full Court. If the case is decided against PETA (on behalf of Naruto), there may still be an interesting dissenting opinion or two. Then it's probably off to see the Wizard—sorry—the US Supreme Court. It was subsequently reported that Dr. Antje Engelhardt had dropped out as one of Naruto's Next Friends, which in hindsight becomes apparent from reading the appeal (March 20, 2016) in which the only Next Friend listed is PETA. This adds a new aspect to the case as a party necessary for standing in the District Court is not participating in the appeal. More important, it has been questioned whether PETA has standing as a sole Next Friend because unlike Dr. Engelhardt (who it is alleged has studied Naruto since his birth) PETA did not allege any relationship with Naruto.

If you are not convinced that trees, as well as monkeys and other animals should be entitled to copyright protection as authors, I hope the theories discussed above have made your day more interesting than your usual reading. Anyone who considers these ideas frivolous must consider where we started—in the Ninth Circuit with *Naruto v. Slater*. On the other hand, lawyers might be able to find clients willing to try new things and start a new trend with loan-out companies for clients who wish to use animals to paint or sing. The purchase and maintenance of an elephant by a client would be quite expensive, so attorneys might want to bone up on how to write a short-term lease agreement for a loan-out company to rent an elephant to a client, just in case. Lawyers will obviously want to include elephant insurance coverage, which may not be that difficult to obtain as a major insurance company is currently advertising on TV that it will insure just about anything.

THE END – NOT QUITE

MONKEY SELFIE UPDATE – Naruto v. Slater

Naruto v. David Slater, the topic and inspiration for the original satire "ENOUGH ABOUT MONKEY SELFIES," came back to life after the appeal to the 9th Circuit Court of Appeals by PETA as "Next Friend" (so says PETA) of Naruto, and was heard by a panel of three appellate court judges on July 12, 2017. For those readers who are interested in viewing and listening to the arguments on appeal, the hearing may be viewed online at [https://www.ca9.uscourts.gov/media/view_video.php?pk_vid=0000011923].

In the meantime other strange things happened. On May 30, 2017 a Request FOR JUDICIAL NOTICE was filed with the Court of Appeals in which EXHIBIT A included a copy of a COMPLAINT-SUMMONS for criminal trespass in the state of New Jersey stating that one Antje Engelhardt on 4/22/2017 rang the doorbell of the residence of PETA attorney Jeffrey Kerr, who told her to leave the premises, after which she allegedly walked into the backyard of the residence. Perhaps she has spent too much time walking wherever she wants to in the jungles of Indonesia in the company of monkeys, or maybe Jeffrey Kerr has spent too much time representing monkeys and doesn't want to talk about them. The COMPLAINT-SUMMONS ironically refers to intent to harass another or cause annoyance or alarm, something that PETA itself would never do, aside from suing a British photographer in a court almost half way around the world (San Francisco) in what appears to be an attempt to gain publicity with a ridiculous theory—that animals can own copyrights.

***

Pending a decision from the Court of Appeals, PETA and Slater entered into a settlement agreement whereby twenty-five percent of any proceeds from the sale of the photos would be donated to charities working to protect the dwindling habitat of crested macaques in Indonesia. Pursuant to the settlement agreement PETA and Slater on September 11, 2017 filed a Joint Motion to Dismiss the Appeal and Vacate the Judgment (of the lower court), which was denied by the Court of Appeals April 13, 2018. The Order (of Denial) stated that the request had been made after a full briefing, extended oral argument, and several months of deliberation during which the Judges of the Court expended considerable resources and sought to resolve and reconcile the various issues involved, and that a decision in this developing area of law would help guide lower courts. Also noted was the fact that the settlement agreement would not bar another attempt to file a new action as Naruto was not a party to the settlement agreement.

[OMITTED – for details see the Unreported Case next]

A three-judge panel of the 9th Circuit Court of Appeals on April 23, 2018 affirmed the dismissal of the case by the District Court. *Naruto v. Slater*, 888 F.3d 418 (9th Cir., 2018). Although the panel held that the animal (Naruto) had constitutional standing, it lacked statutory standing to claim copyright infringement because the Copyright Act does not expressly authorize animals to file copyright infringement suits. It also found that PETA could not represent Naruto as "next friend" because, unlike Dr. Engelhardt, PETA failed to allege meeting the requirement of having a significant relationship with Naruto. However, this was not something that could be remedied by refiling the appeal because the opinion stated that animals cannot have next friend standing.

In his concurring opinion, Judge N. Randy Smith (one of my favorite Judges in the Ninth Circuit) saw through PETA's clever arguments, noting "…when it came down to a possible negative, precedential ruling from the panel, PETA quickly sought to protect the institution, not the claimed real party in interest" [Naruto] and further said, "…PETA made sure to protect itself and with the *Joint Motion* sought to manipulate this court to avoid further negative precedent contrary to its institutional objectives."

After everyone thought that the matter was over, a Ninth Circuit Judge requested a rehearing of the case by the full Circuit, which was rejected August 31, 2018.

THE END

MONKEY'S PETITION BEFORE
9th Circuit Court of Appeals
[Unreported Case]

In an unusual move the 9th Circuit has allowed a last minute petition to be heard in-camera prior to rendering its decision in the appeal of *Naruto v. Slater*. The proceeding is not available online as it was held in-camera with members of the public and press barred. Don't ask how I got it.

***

Three appellate judges for the 9th Circuit sit behind a long bench in a small courtroom in the James R. Browning U.S. Courthouse in San Francisco, California, all dressed in black and looking perplexed. At a table nearby are seated the petitioner and the petitioner's representative.

PETITIONER's REPRESENTATIVE: May it please the court …

PRESIDING JUDGE: You haven't introduced yourself.

PETITIONER's REPRESENTATIVE: I'm sorry Your Honor. My name is Raja.

ASSOCIATE JUDGE: Are you authorized to practice law before this court?

PETITIONER's REPRESENTATIVE: No, Your Honor but I came a long way just to be here and it looks like I got here just in time. It took three months.

ASSOCIATE JUDGE: Three months?

PETITIONER's REPRESENTATIVE: Yes. NARUTO and I live in Indonesia.

ASSOCIATE JUDGE: Why didn't you fly?

PETITIONER's REPRESENTATIVE: They wouldn't let us through airport security in Indonesia, so we took a banana boat. The ride was not very smooth and they ran out of bananas two days before we arrived.

ASSOCIATE JUDGE: While I appreciate that you had a long journey, you are not authorized to practice law in the United States.

VISITING JUDGE: This appeal involves an unusual application of copyright law and I think we should make an exception in this case. I myself did travel across the country to be here so I can appreciate what the PETITIONER's REPRESENTATIVE and the PETITIONER must have endured.

ASSOCIATE JUDGE (to PETITIONER's REPRESENTATIVE): Are you a lawyer in Indonesia?

PETITIONER's REPRESENTATIVE: Not at present.

ASSOCIATE JUDGE: You mean that you are a retired lawyer?

PETITIONER's REPRESENTATIVE: No.

ASSOCIATE JUDGE: Then you must be licensed to practice law in some other country.

PETITIONER's REPRESENTATIVE: I'm afraid not.

ASSOCIATE JUDGE: Then what makes you qualified to represent the PETITIONER?

PETITIONER's REPRESENTATIVE: I'm a mahout.

ASSOCIATE JUDGE: What's that?

PETITIONER's REPRESENTATIVE: A trainer of elephants. I worked in Thailand for many years training elephants to perform in an elephant orchestra, but had to take early retirement because of disability when one of the elephants stepped on my foot. Then I moved back to Indonesia and began helping with monkeys. That's how I got to know NARUTO, even better than Dr. Antje Engelhardt.

VISITING JUDGE: Are you able to communicate with NARUTO?

PETITIONER's REPRESENTATIVE: Definitely.

ASSOCIATE JUDGE: I suppose that you and NARUTO are on a first-named basis.

PETITIONER's REPRESENTATIVE: Don't be ridiculous.

ASSOCIATE JUDGE: This whole lawsuit has been ridiculous from the start.

PRESIDING JUDGE: Be that as it may, we may as well proceed.

PETITIONER's REPRESENTATIVE: I would like to present NARUTO's objections to the way the case has been handled.

VISITING JUDGE: You mean the objections that you have on NARUTO's behalf.

PETITIONER's REPRESENTATIVE: Not at all. NARUTO has made his objections known to me.

ASSOCIATE JUDGE: This, I've gotta see.

PETITIONER's REPRESENTATIVE: You will, but first I wish to demonstrate that NARUTO is capable of manipulating a camera and taking his own selfies unassisted by anyone.

(PETITIONER's REPRESENTATIVE motions to NARUTO, who stands and moves several feet away. PETITIONER's REPRESENTATIVE reaches into his briefcase and pulls out a digital camera; then tosses the camera into the air for NARUTO to catch. NARUTO catches it, starts playing with the camera and pushes the shutter every so often, alternating between smiles and frowns)

PRESIDING JUDGE (to PETITIONER's REPRESENTATIVE): Our time is limited, so please proceed.

(PETITIONER's REPRESENTATIVE unsuccessfully tries to take the camera away from NARUTO. He then pulls a banana from his briefcase and tosses it into the air. NARUTO drops the camera in favor of the banana)

PETITIONER's REPRESENTATIVE: I would like each of you to look at the photos stored in the camera.

(PETITIONER's REPRESENTATIVE hands the camera to the Judge on the left who takes a look and passes the camera along to the other Judges)

ASSOCIATE JUDGE: I don't see any selfies? These are just poor shots, mostly out of focus.

PETITIONER's REPRESENTATIVE: Of course. Most of the selfies shot on David Slater's camera were not worthy of publication, but I have just demonstrated that NARUTO is capable of using a camera to take selfies. If enough photos are taken eventually a good one will result as in the case at hand.

PRESIDING JUDGE: Assuming that NARUTO took the selfie that is the subject of this case, what is it that you are seeking?

PETITIONER's REPRESENTATIVE: I would like to present NARUTO's objections to PETA's representation as his NEXT FRIEND.

PRESIDING JUDGE: What are they?

PETITIONER's REPRESENTATIVE: I would like to question NARUTO.

(The Judges look at each other and shake their heads. PETITIONER's REPRESENTATIVE takes NARUTO by the hand and leads him to a seat up front)

PETITIONER's REPRESENTATIVE: NARUTO, I would like to ask you a few questions.

(NARUTO jumps up and down in the chair and makes faces at the Judges. PETITIONER's REPRESENTATIVE hands NARUTO another banana to calm him down)

ASSOCIATE JUDGE: Am I dreaming?

VISITING JUDGE: No, but this is not any more ridiculous than the copyright issue involved.

PETITIONER's REPRESENTATIVE: NARUTO, do you wish to have PETA represent you as NEXT FRIEND?

(NARUTO responds with a negative answer by shaking his head back and forth)

PETITIONER's REPRESENTATIVE: Why is that?

(NARUTO makes a face and throws the banana peel across the room. PETITIONER's REPRESENTATIVE picks it up and tosses it into a nearby wastebasket. He then opens his wallet and extracts a ten dollar bill, which he hands to NARUTO, who examines it closely)

PETITIONER's REPRESENTATIVE: It's about the money, isn't it?

(NARUTO nods his head to indicate 'yes')

VISITING JUDGE (to PETITIONER's REPRESENTATIVE): You are leading the witness.

ASSOCIATE JUDGE: In addition, the witness is merely shaking his head in response to your questions, not actually answering them.

PETITIONER's REPRESENTATIVE: That is no problem. NARUTO, please answer my questions instead of just shaking your head, okay?

(NARUTO nods his head in agreement)

ASSOCIATE JUDGE: I suppose NARUTO speaks both Indonesian and English.

(The ASSOCIATE JUDGE, amused, hits the table with his fist so hard that his coffee cup spills over)

PETITIONER's REPRESENTATIVE: Only English.

ASSOCIATE JUDGE: Did he learn English in high school in Indonesia?

PETITIONER's REPRESENTATIVE: Of course not. NARUTO learned English during his three month voyage on the banana boat. One of the crew was a former teacher of English as a second language.

PRESIDING JUDGE (to PETITIONER's REPRESENTATIVE): Let's stop wasting time. Proceed with your questions.

PETITIONER's REPRESENTATIVE (to NARUTO): NARUTO, do you wish to have PETA represent you as NEXT FRIEND?

NARUTO (speaking English with an unusual accent): Where is Dr. Engelhardt?

(The three Judges react with astonishment)

PETITIONER's REPRESENTATIVE: I am sorry to tell you that Dr. Engelhardt is no longer participating as a NEXT FRIEND in this appeal.

NARUTO: Bollocks.

PETITIONER's REPRESENTATIVE: Please, NARUTO, you must be more respectful in Court.

NARUTO: Sorry.

PETITIONER's REPRESENTATIVE: I ask you again, do you wish to have PETA represent you as NEXT FRIEND?

NARUTO: No.

PETITIONER's REPRESENTATIVE: Why is that?

NARUTO: They plan to spend my royalties not only on me, but also on my relatives and other macaques in the community and their habitat.

PETITIONER's REPRESENTATIVE: What's wrong with that?

NARUTO: It's my money, mine, only mine.

VISITING JUDGE: That's a valid point, assuming that NARUTO owns the copyright to his selfie. If PETA, or anyone, were to be appointed by the Court to collect NARUTO's royalties, it would create a fiduciary relationship and the money would have to be held in trust strictly for the benefit of NARUTO, not others.

ASSOCIATE JUDGE: I agree, purely from a theoretical viewpoint. Spending trust funds on other monkeys would be a clear violation of fiduciary duty.

PRESIDING JUDGE: That certainly is a valid concern and will be taken into account.

PETITIONER's REPRESENTATIVE (to NARUTO): Do you have any more objections?

NARUTO: I don't want to pay some agent 10% to collect my royalties or 33% to any lawyers.

ASSOCIATE JUDGE (to NARUTO): That may be of concern to you, but it is not relevant to whether or not PETA should continue to represent you as NEXT FRIEND in this appeal.

(The ASSOCIATE JUDGE slaps himself on the forehead)

ASSOCIATE JUDGE: I don't believe this. I am talking to a monkey.

NARUTO: I'm a macaque, not a monkey.

PRESIDING JUDGE (to PETITIONER's REPRESENTATIVE): Any more questions?

PETITIONER's REPRESENTATIVE: No, that is all.

ASSOCIATE JUDGE (to PRESIDING JUDGE): I hope the record of this hearing will be sealed.

PRESIDING JUDGE: The case will be submitted for decision, but the record of this hearing will definitely be sealed.

VISITING JUDGE: Thank God. If this ever got out.…

<u>THE END</u>

[See previous article for subsequent events]

SOLICITOR GENERAL IN A COW PASTURE

NOTE: Procedure in the United States District Courts is not necessarily as portrayed in this play, which is a follow on to the recent article about *Naruto v. Slater* entitled "ENOUGH ABOUT MONKEY SELFIES."

(The scene is a courtroom, not your ordinary one, but an outdoor setting in a cow pasture. The judge sits on a rail fence, squirming uncomfortably. To one side is a sign on a stick leaning against the fence: U.S. District Court. On the other side is a pine tree, the Plaintiff, with an abandoned piece of sheet metal at the base of the tree; behind it are two smaller trees. In front of the judge sits a large metal drum, upon which a gavel rests. A red barn is in the background and the hot sun is shining above)

JUDGE: *Conifer v. the United States.* This is an action against the U.S. Copyright Office filed by a tree.

(The JUDGE pauses, shakes his head)

JUDGE: Is that right Counsellor, a tree?

PLAINTIFF's ATTORNEY: That is correct, unusual as it may be.

JUDGE: Not really; after a while you have seen everything.

(The JUDGE looks around and notices the trees off to the side)

JUDGE: Which one is the Plaintiff?

PLAINTIFF's ATTORNEY (pointing): The tall one with the drooping branches, nearest the fence.

JUDGE: The complaint alleges that the Defendant has refused to file copyright applications for three works created by the Plaintiff, as musical compositions and as sound recordings, on the ground that an author of copyrightable material must be a human being. Defendant filed a motion to dismiss on the grounds that Plaintiff has no standing to file a suit, citing *Naruto v. David Slater*, a 2016 case in which a District Court in San Francisco held that a monkey cannot be the author and owner of a selfie— a photograph of the monkey taken by itself. Defendant also filed a motion to dismiss for failure to state a claim upon which relief may be granted, contending that Plaintiff's material consists merely of sounds that are not subject to copyright protection.

PLAINTIFF's ATTORNEY: Your Honor, may it please the court …

JUDGE: I prefer "Your Excellency."

PLAINTIFF's ATTORNEY: Your Excellency …

(*pause*)

JUDGE: Your Excellency, what?

PLAINTIFF's ATTORNEY: I was about to say …

JUDGE: Well, get on with it! Do you think I can sit on this rail fence all day?

PLAINTIFF's ATTORNEY: Sorry, Your Honor.

JUDGE: Your what?

PLAINTIFF's ATTORNEY: Your Excellency. Defendant's Reliance on *Naruto v. Slater* is premature at this time.

JUDGE: How is that?

PLAINTIFF's ATTORNEY: The case is on appeal in the Ninth Circuit, which has been known to toss copyright law on its head, and PETA (acting as Next Friend of Naruto) is very determined to pursue the case, all the way to the Supreme Court and beyond.

JUDGE: Where would beyond be?

PLAINTIFF's ATTORNEY: Just a figure of speech, but PETA is no doubt determined.

JUDGE: True enough.

PLAINTIFF's ATTORNEY: In any event, *Naruto v. Slater* is not on point, because it involves alleged copyright infringement. The instant case is concerned with copyright registration.

SOLICITOR GENERAL: I do not know why we have to hear this case out here in the sticks.

JUDGE: Careful, sonny ... In case you have not noticed, the Plaintiff is a tree and can hardly walk to California, unless you believe in Monty Python's sketch *The Walking Tree of Dahomey*. We accommodate plaintiffs with disabilities here.

PLAINTIFF's ATTORNEY: Unlike you lazy bozos in Washington.

SOLICITOR GENERAL: I object, Your Honor.

JUDGE: It's Your Excellency. The next one who says "Your Honor," is in contempt of court.

(*Some cows pass by on their way to the barn. The* JUDGE *bangs his gavel on the metal drum*)

JUDGE: Bailiff, clear the court.

(*The* BAILIFF *shoes the cows away, toward the barn. The* JUDGE *again bangs the gavel on the metal drum—several times—as the cows exit, this time giving the sounds a musical twist*)

PLAINTIFF's ATTORNEY: That has a nice ring to it, Your Excellency, very musical.

JUDGE: Thank you.

PLAINTIFF's ATTORNEY: You might want to record it; I can recommend a good agent.

JUDGE: Do you really think so?

SOLICITOR GENERAL: I object.

JUDGE: You don't like my drum music?

SOLICITOR GENERAL: That is not what I meant, Your Honor.

JUDGE: Did I hear you correctly?

SOLICITOR GENERAL: I said Your Excellency; I'm sure that's what I said.

JUDGE: You did not.

SOLICITOR GENERAL: I meant to say Your Excellency.

JUDGE: Too late. Bailiff, this man is in contempt.

(*The* BAILIFF *approaches and places a dunce cap on the head of the* SOLICITOR GENERAL. *The dunce cap is a little too large and the* BAILIFF *tries to help the* SOLICITOR GENERAL *adjust it*)

BAILIFF: There is a twenty-five cent deposit for the cap.

(*The* SOLICITOR GENERAL *puts his hands in his pockets and comes up empty*)

SOLICITOR GENERAL: No change. Will you take a check? I don't usually travel with cash.

BAILIFF (to JUDGE): Wants to know if we will take a check for the deposit.

JUDGE: The Court will exercise its discretion and generously waive the twenty-five cent deposit.

(*The* BAILIFF *turns to leave and accidentally steps on the* SOLICITOR GENERAL's *shoes*)

SOLICITOR GENERAL: These shoes are brand new. Do you have any idea how much they cost?

BAILIFF: No, I wear boots.

JUDGE (to SOLICITOR GENERAL): The United States of America is wasting the Court's time. Do you have anything more to say?

SOLICITOR GENERAL: I have not even started, Your Excellency. I wish to file an objection to the statement made by Plaintiff's Attorney.

JUDGE: What is it that you find objectionable?

SOLICITOR GENERAL: The whole thing is insulting.

JUDGE: You will have to be more specific. Are you objecting to lazy or bozos?

SOLICITOR GENERAL: Both.

JUDGE: Objection overruled as to lazy; it is common knowledge that Congress has not accomplished much of anything for quite some time.

SOLICITOR GENERAL: What?

JUDGE: Counsellor, are you familiar with Rule 201?

SOLICITOR GENERAL: Which one?

JUDGE: Rule 201 of the Federal Rules of Evidence. It provides that a U.S. District Court may take judicial notice of a fact not subject to reasonable dispute and generally know. Do you have any evidence to offer to refute the statement that Congress is lazy?

SOLICITOR GENERAL: Are you kidding?

JUDGE: Objection overruled, as to lazy.

SOLICITOR GENERAL: I still object to bozos.

JUDGE: Because the word bozos is modified by the adjective lazy, it cannot be separated from lazy in this context; objection also overruled as to bozos. You may sit down.

(*The* SOLICITOR GENERAL *looks around, finds nothing to sit on and steps back*)

JUDGE (to PLAINTIFF's ATTORNEY): Are you ready to make an opening statement?

PLAINTIFF's ATTORNEY: Yes Your Excellency. Plaintiff has filed this action to require the U.S. Copyright Office to register three musical works composed by the Plaintiff. The Plaintiff will call a witness to testify that some sounds made by trees—and in particular the Plaintiff's—are considered to be music, thus subject to copyright as musical compositions, as well as sound recordings, whether or not considered as music. The Defendant's refusal is contrary to law.

JUDGE (to SOLICITOR GENERAL): Counsellor, do you wish to make an opening statement for the Defendant.

SOLICITOR GENERAL: I do not think it is necessary to take any more of the Court's time, and I must get back to Washington for an important meeting.

(*The* SOLICITOR GENERAL *looks at his watch*)

JUDGE: Was that a yes or a no?

SOLICITOR GENERAL: No opening statement. Instead, I make a motion to dismiss for lack of standing, as Plaintiff is not a human being.

JUDGE: I do not see that requirement in the copyright statute. Motion denied.

(*The* JUDGE *hits the metal drum with his gavel*)

SOLICITOR GENERAL: Then, I would like to make an opening statement.

JUDGE: Too late.

SOLICITOR GENERAL: The Rules of Civil Procedure of the Federal District Courts allow …

JUDGE: We have a shorter version out here sonny—in the sticks as you called it.

SOLICITOR GENERAL: I need to make a phone call.

JUDGE: Fine, but you will have to step outside the courtroom. Court will recess for ten minutes.

SOLICITOR GENERAL: We are in a cow pasture, not a courthouse.

JUDGE: Bailiff, would you set up the perimeter of the courtroom?

(*The* BAILIFF *enters the barn and returns with a two-wheeled white line marker, which he pushes around to set off a rectangle that marks the interior of the courtroom, ending at the rail fence. The* BAILIFF *looks down as he pushes the machine, diligently trying to make the lines straight. Near the edge of the proposed boundary, the* SOLICITOR GENERAL *is trying to make a call on his cell phone, but doesn't notice the approaching* BAILIFF)

SOLICITOR GENERAL (into phone): No, I am not calling from a secure phone; I am calling from a cow pasture.

(*The* BAILIFF, *eyes on the ground, pushes the machine over the* SOLICITOR GENERAL's *right foot, covering the shoe with white chalk*)

SOLICITOR GENERAL: Shit.

(pause)

SOLICITOR GENERAL (continuing - into phone): No, I wasn't talking to you.

(pause)

SOLICITOR GENERAL (continuing): Hello … hello … hello …

(*The* BAILIFF *reaches the fence, finishing his task, returns the chalk machine to the barn and reappears*)

JUDGE: Bailiff.

BAILIFF: Court is back in session.

SOLICITOR GENERAL: I was disconnected; I didn't finish my call.

JUDGE (to SOLICITOR GENERAL): Maybe you did not hear the Bailiff, but Court is back in session. Would you like a recess until tomorrow morning so you can go into town and buy a hearing aid?

SOLICITOR GENERAL: No, no. Everything is fine.

(*He looks at his watch*)

SOLICITOR GENERAL: If we could just speed things up, maybe I can make the five o'clock train back to Washington.

JUDGE: Give your watch to the Bailiff to hold so you can concentrate on the case.

SOLICITOR GENERAL: It's very expensive.

(*He suddenly covers the watch with his right hand*)

JUDGE: A Rolex?

SOLICITOR GENERAL: Certainly not. It's a Patek Philippe.

PLAINTIFF's ATTORNEY: The Department of Justice must pay pretty well. I must have the wrong job.

JUDGE: Me too. Are there any vacancies at the DOJ?

SOLICITOR GENERAL: I will just put the watch in my pocket if that will be OK, Your Excellency.

(*He takes the watch off and puts it in his pants pocket*)

JUDGE (to PLAINTIFF's ATTORNEY): Let us proceed. Counsellor, you may argue the Plaintiff's case.

PLAINTIFF's ATTORNEY: Copyright law provides two distinct types of protection for musical works, one for musical compositions and another for sound recordings. A musical composition often contains lyrics in addition to melody, but does not always have lyrics.

BAILIFF: What's lyrics?

JUDGE: Bailiff, your duties do not include asking questions.

BAILIFF: Sorry, Your Excellency.

PLAINTIFF's ATTORNEY: Lyrics, for the benefit of the Bailiff, are the words that accompany a song, but not all compositions have words, as in Plaintiff's case. Copyright results the moment the words and/or melody are fixed in a tangible form, such as saved on a computer disk or printed as a hard copy, etc.

JUDGE: We do not use etcetera in this courtroom, Counsellor. Bailiff, please strike etcetera from the record.

PLAINTIFF's ATTORNEY: When a sound recording is made of the musical composition, a copyright results in the recording, which is separate from the copyright in the musical work itself.

SOLICITOR GENERAL: Aha! Perhaps you could explain how your client created a copyright in its work by reducing it to writing, prior to recording it. Maybe he wrote it down with a branch.

(*The* SOLICITOR GENERAL *laughs at his own joke*)

SOLICITOR GENERAL (continuing): Perhaps we could have a demonstration.

JUDGE (to SOLICITOR GENERAL): Counsellor, approach the bench.

SOLICITOR GENERAL: Who me?

JUDGE: Who me what?

SOLICITOR GENERAL: Who me, Your Excellency?

JUDGE: That's better.

(*He motions with his index finger and the* SOLICITOR GENERAL *comes forward*)

SOLICITOR GENERAL: Here I am.

(*He points at the steel drum*)

SOLICITOR GENERAL: I guess this is the bench.

JUDGE: Lucky guess.

(*He pounds the gavel on the drum so loud that the* SOLICITOR GENERAL *jumps*)

SOLICITOR GENERAL: Did I say something wrong?

JUDGE: No jokes in the courtroom, got that?

SOLICITOR GENERAL: Absolutely.

JUDGE: Absolutely, what?

SOLICITOR GENERAL: Absolutely, Your Excellency.

JUDGE: Another thing. Why are you dressed up like a funeral director?

SOLICITOR GENERAL: I didn't realize that we would be in the middle of a … I mean outdoors.

JUDGE: Very well. Let's continue.

(*The* SOLICITOR GENERAL *moves back and the* PLAINTIFF's ATTORNEY *steps forward*)

PLAINTIFF's ATTORNEY: As everyone knows, or at least almost everyone knows …

(*He looks at the* SOLICITOR GENERAL)

PLAINTIFF's ATTORNEY (continuing): If a musical composition is not already in writing, it becomes fixed in a tangible form when recorded the first time it is sung or played. Two copyrights come into existence simultaneously, one for the original musical composition and another for the sound recording. It is not necessary that a musical composition be in written form before it is performed and recorded.

SOLICITOR GENERAL: I know that. I was just exploring a point.

PLAINTIFF's ATTORNEY: Naturally, a point that I just explained away.

JUDGE: Can we continue?

PLAINTIFF's ATTORNEY: Upon the recording of Plaintiff's musical composition, a separate copyright was created in the musical work and another in the sound recording.

SOLICITOR GENERAL: Objection. It has not yet been established that the sounds allegedly made by Plaintiff are actually music.

PLAINTIFF's ATTORNEY: Your Excellency, I am about to establish that.

JUDGE: Objection overruled.

PLAINTIFF's ATTORNEY: I call my first witness.

(*He whistles and a black bird swoops down from nowhere and perches on the rail fence*)

SOLICITOR GENERAL: You are calling a crow as a witness. Is this, a joke?

(*The black bird flies above the head of the* SOLICITOR GENERAL *and hovers, flapping its wings*)

RAVEN: I am a raven, not a crow, you idiot.

(*Then it flies back to settle on the rail fence*)

SOLICITOR GENERAL: Your Excellency, I object to the word … never mind.

(*He looks at his wrist, having forgotten that the watch is in his pocket*)

JUDGE (to RAVEN): Take the witness stand.

(*The* BAILIFF *wheels over a large wheelbarrow and the* RAVEN *flies over and perches on the edge of a handle*)

JUDGE: Bailiff, swear in the witness.

BAILIFF: I forgot to bring a Bible.

JUDGE: Just proceed without one.

BAILIFF (to RAVEN): Hold up your right … never mind.

PLAINTIFF's ATTORNEY: Raven, are you familiar with the Plaintiff?

RAVEN: Yes.

PLAINTIFF's ATTORNEY: What is your relationship?

RAVEN: Well, I often rest on its branches and it never complains or tries to shake me off.

PLAINTIFF's ATTORNEY: Would you say that you were friends?

SOLICITOR GENERAL: Aha! Your Excellency, I move to have Raven declared as a hostile witness.

JUDGE: And what purpose will that serve?

SOLICITOR GENERAL: Well … uh …

JUDGE: Time's up. Motion denied.

PLAINTIFF's ATTORNEY: Raven, are you familiar with the sounds that Plaintiff makes?

RAVEN: Of course; I hear them several times a day.

PLAINTIFF's ATTORNEY: Would you consider them to be music?

SOLICITOR GENERAL: Objection. It has not been established that Raven is an expert witness in the field of music.

PLAINTIFF's ATTORNEY: I will stipulate that Raven is not an expert music witness, but I merely ask the Court to hear his testimony as a personal opinion, by one who has spent more time in the woods listening to the sounds of trees and birds than any music professor or graduate of The Julliard School in New York.

JUDGE: Very well. Subject to the stipulation that Raven is not an expert witness, you may proceed.

PLAINTIFF's ATTORNEY: I repeat; would you consider Plaintiff's sounds to be music?

RAVEN: Kraaa, kraaa, kraaa.

PLAINTIFF's ATTORNEY: I beg your pardon.

RAVEN: Sorry, English is not my first language. Sometimes I forget. I meant to say most of them.

SOLICITOR GENERAL: Objection to most of them.

JUDGE: Objection sustained.

(*He hits his gavel on the steel drum*)

JUDGE (to PLAINTIFF's ATTORNEY): Counsellor, your question will have to be more specific.

PLAINTIFF's ATTORNEY: I would like to offer into evidence this CD, which the Court and Raven may listen to, followed by Raven's personal opinion as to whether the sounds constitute music. The CD is attached to Plaintiff's complaint as an Exhibit.

JUDGE: Very well, you may proceed.

PLAINTIFF's ATTORNEY: There are three musical works on the CD, Your Excellency.

(*The* PLAINTIFF's ATTORNEY *sets up a battery operated CD player on the drum and all gather round to listen, their facial expressions varying from time to time. The first one emits various sounds, including branches creaking and swaying in the wind, leaves rustling and branches snapping back, returning to position as squirrels jump from one branch to the next*)

SOLICITOR GENERAL: Your Excellency, this is not a recording of a musical composition, and cannot possibly qualify for copyright protection. It is just loud sounds, and basic ones at that.

PLAINTIFF's ATTORNEY: Music is not the only sound that can be recorded.

SOLICITOR GENERAL: Yes, but this case is about the Plaintiff's alleged copyright in a recorded musical composition, not the recording of basic non-musical sounds.

PLAINTIFF's ATTORNEY: I stand corrected, a rare occurrence.

SOLICITOR GENERAL: The sounds are not music and have no artistic quality at all.

PLAINTIFF's ATTORNEY: Artistic merit is not a requirement for copyright. I cite *Hein v. Harris* 175 F. 875 (1910), affirmed by the Second Circuit in 1923, in which Judge Learned Hand stated that the lack of originality and musical merit in songs is of no consequence. The case involved copyright infringement, in which Judge Hand compared *Arab Love Song* to *I Think I Hear a Woodpecker*.

SOLICITOR GENERAL: Nevertheless, a musical work must contain a sufficient amount of creative expression to be copyrightable. I cite the *Compendium of U. S. Copyright Office Practices, Third Edition* (2014).

PLAINTIFF's ATTORNEY: I object. The *Compendium* is not a law; it is merely an internal document used by the U.S. Copyright Office as a guide in registering works for copyright, or more precisely what the Copyright Office is willing to register.

SOLICITOR GENERAL: I object to your objection.

JUDGE (to SOLICITOR GENERAL): Counsellor, could you give the Court a more specific citation from this *Compendium*?

SOLICITOR GENERAL: Certainly, Your Excellency.

(*He opens his briefcase, pulls out a thick book and starts thumbing through it*)

PLAINTIFF's ATTORNEY: Are you going to read the whole thing? How many pages is it, anyway?

SOLICITOR GENERAL: 1,288 pages, but it won't take very long; I have bookmarked several sections.

(*He starts flipping through the book, but it is thick and heavy and he drops it; some of the bookmarks fall out, but he scrambles to pick them up, first grabbing the book*)

JUDGE: Looks like this is going to take you some time. Counsellor, why don't you have a seat in the witness box?

(*He looks at the* BAILIFF *and motions with his hand. The* BAILIFF *moves the wheelbarrow toward the* SOLICITOR GENERAL *and scoops him up into it; the book falls to the ground. The* BAILIFF *picks up the book and remaining bookmarks and hands them to the* SOLICITOR GENERAL)

JUDGE: Bailiff, why don't you and I take a break and go have a cold beer. Court is in recess for fifteen minutes.

(*They walk off as the* SOLICITOR GENERAL *attempts to get out of the wheelbarrow; unsuccessful, he sits back and flips through the pages, inserts a bookmark here and there, and continues looking*)

SOLICITOR GENERAL (mumbling): It must be here somewhere.

(*The* JUDGE *and the* BAILIFF *return in fifteen minutes more or less. The* BAILIFF *carries a ceramic beer stein, which he hands to the* SOLICITOR GENERAL)

SOLICITOR GENERAL: Thank you.

(*He takes a sip and stops*)

SOLICITOR GENERAL: What is this? I was expecting a cold beer.

BAILIFF: It's lemonade.

SOLICITOR GENERAL: Really, it's somewhat weak.

BAILIFF: You can't drink alcohol in the courtroom.

JUDGE: Court's in session. Counsellor, have you found your citation?

SOLICITOR GENERAL: Yes, Your Excellency. Section 803.3(A) of the *Compendium*.

JUDGE: Counsellor, you must stand to address the Court.

(*The* SOLICITOR GENERAL *struggles to get out of the wheelbarrow without success*)

JUDGE: Bailiff, help the Solicitor General out of the witness box.

(*The* BAILIFF *tips the wheelbarrow forward and the* SOLICITOR GENERAL *falls out)*

SOLICITOR GENERAL (dusting himself off): My new suit; it's all dirty.

JUDGE: No problem. You don't have to look presentable out here. Let's have your citation.

SOLICITOR GENERAL: I just gave it to you.

JUDGE: You were not before the court when you spoke.

BAILIFF: You were in the witness box.

SOLICITOR GENERAL: Very well, I again cite Section 803.3(A) of the *Compendium*.

JUDGE: Counsellor, the *Compendium* has no standing as law, although the Court may give due deference to the opinions of the U.S. Copyright Office if you wish to offer the *Compendium* into evidence.

(*The* SOLICITOR GENERAL *hands the Compendium to the* BAILIFF)

JUDGE: So entered.

SOLICITOR GENERAL: I request that the Court rule that the first so called composition is not subject to copyright because it has only basic sounds that are not music; there is absolutely no creative expression whatsoever.

JUDGE: Denied. The motion is redundant as worded.

SOLICITOR GENERAL: What?

JUDGE: Absolutely and whatsoever are redundant. You can use one or the other, not both.

BAILIFF (to SOLICITOR GENERAL): His Excellency was an English teacher before he became a judge.

SOLICITOR GENERAL: I don't believe it.

BAILIFF: It's true.

SOLICITOR GENERAL: I wasn't talking to you.

BAILIFF: Talking to yourself again, are you; I had better write that down.

(*The* SOLICITOR GENERAL *turns away and ignores the* BAILIFF)

JUDGE: Counsellor, do you wish to restate your motion?

SOLICITOR GENERAL: Yes, Your Excellency. I make a motion for the Court to rule that the first so-called musical work is not subject to copyright protection as a musical composition or as a sound recording because the sounds are not musical and have no creative expression whatsoever.

JUDGE: Motion granted. Bailiff, play the next one.

(*He bangs the gavel. The next recording includes branches creaking and swaying in the background, together with the sound of pine cones dropping and repeatedly landing on an abandoned piece of sheet metal at the base of the tree*)

SOLICITOR GENERAL: I would like to…

PLAINTIFF's ATTORNEY: Objection.

SOLICITOR GENERAL: You can't object; I haven't said anything yet.

PLAINTIFF's ATTORNEY: My witness should be recalled first.

JUDGE: Objection sustained. Bailiff, move the witness stand back over here.

(*The* BAILIFF *moves the wheelbarrow close to the fence and the* RAVEN *hops back on one of the handles*)

JUDGE: Raven, you are still under oath. Counsellor, you may proceed.

PLAINTIFF's ATTORNEY: Raven, you just listened to the Plaintiff's second musical composition.

SOLICITOR GENERAL: Objection. Counsel is leading the witness. It has not been established that these sounds are musical.

JUDGE: Sustained.

PLAINTIFF's ATTORNEY: Raven, in your personal, non-expert opinion, what do you consider the sounds you just heard to be?

RAVEN: It's music to my ears.

SOLICITOR GENERAL: Nonsense. There is no creativity to it.

PLAINTIFF's ATTORNEY: Not true at all. The tree, unassisted and by its own action, is dropping pine cones (onto a piece of metal) at repeated but intermittent intervals, creating a syncopated rhythm, much like a drum solo.

SOLICITOR GENERAL: It is not music in my opinion.

PLAINTIFF's ATTORNEY: Objection. You are not an expert witness.

JUDGE: Sustained.

SOLICITOR GENERAL: But I do have a right to a personal opinion, just like your witness.

PLAINTIFF's ATTORNEY: Of course, but do you actually listen to music?

SOLICITOR GENERAL: Everyone does.

PLAINTIFF's ATTORNEY: That's not an answer. It's a yes or no question.

SOLICITOR GENERAL: Yes.

PLAINTIFF's ATTORNEY: What is your favorite type of music?

SOLICITOR GENERAL: Classical—chamber music in particular.

PLAINTIFF's ATTORNEY: Something by Haydn or Mozart I suppose. Do you have a preference?

SOLICITOR GENERAL: Haydn's string quartet Op. 20 … Say, why are we talking about what kind of music I like?

JUDGE: Counsellor, is this going anywhere relevant to the case?

PLAINTIFF's ATTORNEY: Yes, as my next question will show.

JUDGE: Very well, proceed.

PLAINTIFF's ATTORNEY (to SOLICITOR GENERAL): Do you like ragtime music?

SOLICITOR GENERAL: Are you kidding?

PLAINTIFF's ATTORNEY: I take that as a no.

SOLICITOR GENERAL: It is just a lot of unorganized noise flying about in the air.

PLAINTIFF's ATTORNEY: You apparently agree with Judge Learned Hand's opinion of ragtime.

SOLICITOR GENERAL: I suppose so.

PLAINTIFF's ATTORNEY: Then, you must agree with Judge Hand's statement in *Hein v. Harris* that copyright law protects musical works without any merit or originality. So, what's your problem with a copyright for Plaintiff's second work?

SOLICITOR GENERAL: That was a trick question.

JUDGE: Yes, but well done.

BAILIFF: You stepped in it that time.

JUDGE: Bailiff, you need not state the obvious.

BAILIFF: Sorry, Your Excellency.

SOLICITOR GENERAL: I ask the Court to rule that the sounds in the second work reveal no creativity and it is not copyrightable, either as a musical composition or sound recording.

JUDGE: I will reserve judgment for now, but the Plaintiff's composition does resemble a drum solo. Bailiff, play the last composition.

(*The* BAILIFF *plays the third work, predominantly a whistling sound, shrill at times, with a wide range that keeps changing as the wind blows through a hole in a large branch; birds sing in the background*)

PLAINTIFF's ATTORNEY: Raven, please give us your opinion, not as an expert witness but as a personal opinion, as to the merits of the composition we just enjoyed.

SOLICITOR GENERAL: Objection to enjoyed.

PLAINTIFF's ATTORNEY: You didn't enjoy it?

SOLICITOR GENERAL: That's not the point. Enjoyed gives undue merit as to the quality of the sounds.

JUDGE: Sustained.

PLAINTIFF's ATTORNEY: Raven, please give us your opinion, not as an expert witness but as a personal opinion, as to the merits of the composition we just listened to, whether or not you enjoyed it.

RAVEN: I especially liked the birds singing in the background.

SOLICITOR GENERAL: Aha! If, and I say if, the Plaintiff is an author, then it follows that the birds singing in the background are joint authors. They have not been included as plaintiffs so I ask for dismissal on the basis that not all necessary parties are before the Court.

PLAINTIFF's ATTORNEY: Objection. The birds singing in the background are not making a substantial creative contribution to the work, so they cannot be joint authors. They are similar to non-featured background singers who appear with a lead singer; they are not joint authors.

JUDGE (to SOLICITOR GENERAL): You have not established that the birds are necessary parties under Rule 19(a). Dismissal denied.

PLAINTIFF's ATTORNEY: Raven, aside from the birds singing in the background, did you find the composition musical, in your personal opinion?

RAVEN: Very much so.

PLAINTIFF's ATTORNEY: Creative?

SOLICITOR GENERAL: Objection.

JUDGE: Sustained.

PLAINTIFF's ATTORNEY: No further questions.

(*The* RAVEN *flaps its wings and rises a bit into the air*)

JUDGE: Just a minute, Raven.

(*He turns to the* SOLICITOR GENERAL)

JUDGE: Did you wish to cross-examine the witness?

SOLICITOR GENERAL: By all means.

(*The* RAVEN *perches on the wheelbarrow handles, jumping back and forth from one to the other*)

SOLICITOR GENERAL: Raven, do you spend all of your time resting on the branches of the Plaintiff.

RAVEN: No, I fly quite a wide area and hang about here and there.

SOLICITOR GENERAL: So you are familiar with the sounds of many different trees.

RAVEN: Yes.

SOLICITOR GENERAL: Would you describe most of these sounds as noise rather than music?

RAVEN: Not really.

SOLICITOR GENERAL: Objection.

JUDGE: You can't object to your own question.

SOLICITOR GENERAL: Do you know what a scherzo is, or a sonata?

RAVEN: Italian food?

SOLICITOR GENERAL: What about Schumann and Mendelssohn's fugues?

RAVEN: Did they get in a fight?

SOLICITOR GENERAL: Have you ever listened to the piano concertos of Franz Liszt or Frederic Chopin.

RAVEN: I've never seen a piano out here in the cow pasture, much less heard one. It would not be a good idea, especially in the rainy season.

SOLICITOR GENERAL: Never mind. Let's try one last time. Are you familiar with Samuel Barber's Adagio for Strings or Ludwig van Beethoven's Symphony No. 9 in D Minor?

RAVEN: Can't say that I am.

SOLICITOR GENERAL: Then you are not familiar with the sound of real music?

PLAINTIFF's ATTORNEY: Objection. Raven has obviously heard what the Solicitor General would have to concede is "real" music. Farm hands whistle and sing as they go about their daily choirs, sometimes playing music on their radios outdoors. Everyone knows that cows are more relaxed and produce more milk when listening to soothing music.

BAILIFF: Not everyone.

PLAINTIFF's ATTORNEY: Almost everyone. I can hear music coming from the barn right now.

SOLICITOR GENERAL (shaking his head): It is Mozart's Concerto for Flute and Harp in D Major.

RAVEN: If you say so. I didn't know what it was but I have heard it before while sitting atop the barn.

JUDGE: Any further questions?

SOLICITOR GENERAL: What good would it do?

JUDGE: Bailiff, play that third composition again. I want to focus more on the whistling sounds and tune out the birds in the background.

(*They all listen again*)

RAVEN: Sounds like music to me.

SOLICITOR GENERAL: No one asked you. Your Excellency, I ask that the court strike this statement of the crow from the record.

RAVEN: Who you calling a crow, bozo?

(*The* RAVEN *flies above, buzzing round the head of the* SOLICITOR GENERAL, *which fortunately is protected by the dunce cap. However, we hear a SPLAT just before the* RAVEN *flies off*)

JUDGE: Order in the Court.

(*He pounds his gavel on the metal drum repeatedly*)

JUDGE (continuing): I will reserve judgment for now, but the whistling sound does resemble music.

SOLICITOR GENERAL: With all due respect, Your Excellency, the wind would seem to be the author of the whistling sound, not the tree, or alternatively a joint author.

JUDGE (to SOLICITOR GENERAL): Assuming that the Plaintiff, a tree, qualifies as an author, does the wind consider itself as a joint author?

SOLICITOR GENERAL: I have no idea.

JUDGE: You brought it up—the concept of joint authors. If you don't know, are you prepared to present a witness?

SOLICITOR GENERAL: Do you mean the wind?

JUDGE: Obviously.

(*The* SOLICITOR GENERAL *takes off the dunce cap and waives it in the air in total frustration*)

JUDGE: Bailiff.

(*The* BAILIFF *moves forward, takes the dunce cap by the edges and places it back on the* SOLICITOR GENERAL's *head, very securely*)

SOLICITOR GENERAL: Ouch, that hurts.

JUDGE: Are you making a complaint about the Bailiff? He's my wife's cousin.

SOLICITOR GENERAL: No, absolutely not … Your Excellency.

JUDGE: Now, where were we?

SOLICITOR GENERAL (to himself): In a cow pasture in the middle of nowhere.

JUDGE: What's that Counsellor? You will have to speak up.

SOLICITOR GENERAL: Nothing, Your Excellency; just mumbling to myself. I don't recall what I said.

JUDGE: Bailiff, make a note. Defendant's counsel talks to himself and has memory problems.

(*The* SOLICITOR GENERAL *raises his arm to look at his watch, which is not there*)

JUDGE: I hope you are not looking to see what time it is?

(*The* SOLICITOR GENERAL *starts scratching his wrist vigorously*)

SOLICITOR GENERAL: No Your Excellency. I just got a sudden itch.

JUDGE: Very well. Let's continue.

SOLICITOR GENERAL: I would like to make a motion for dismissal for failure to join a necessary party.

PLAINTIFF's ATTORNEY: You already made that motion.

SOLICITOR GENERAL: That was for the birds.

PLAINTIFF's ATTORNEY: Certainly was.

SOLICITOR GENERAL: I am referring to the wind as a joint author this time. I move for dismissal with respect to the third composition for failure to join a necessary party.

JUDGE: Do you have any evidence to introduce that the wind intended to be a joint author?

SOLICITOR GENERAL: No.

JUDGE: Motion to dismiss for failure to join a necessary party denied.

SOLICITOR GENERAL: The wind does not really need to be a joint author because the wind created the whistling sounds, not the Plaintiff.

JUDGE: Maybe it is time to question the Plaintiff.

PLAINTIFF's ATTORNEY: As the Court has already noted, the Plaintiff has a physical disability (being rooted to the ground), and cannot take the witness stand.

SOLICITOR GENERAL: No one is going to believe this when I get back to Washington.

BAILIFF: Don't tell anyone.

JUDGE: If the Plaintiff cannot come to the courthouse, the Court will go to the Plaintiff. Bailiff, redraw the perimeter of the courtroom.

(*The* BAILIFF *goes to the barn, returns with the chalk machine and pushes it along to enclose the Plaintiff within the boundaries of the courtroom. The* JUDGE *slides down the rail fence, sits closer to the* PLAINTIFF, *shaded by its* branches, *and waits for the* BAILIFF *to return*)

JUDGE: Swear in the witness.

(*The* BAILIFF *holds up a branch of the tree, looks around and drops it*)

PLAINTIFF's ATTORNEY: I will take the oath on behalf of my client.

JUDGE: That will not be necessary. We will just consider the witness sworn.

JUDGE (to SOLICITOR GENERAL): Counsellor, do you wish to ask the witness any questions.

SOLICITOR GENERAL (to PLAINTIFF): I would like to know if you did anything to cause the sounds that we heard in the last recording. If not, the sole creator must be the wind.

(*He stares at the tree, then looks around at everyone else*)

SOLICITOR GENERAL (continuing): I must be crazy. I am talking to a tree.

BAILIFF: Better than talking to yourself.

SOLICITOR GENERAL: I make a motion for summary judgment to dismiss works two and three on the basis that the Plaintiff itself took no action in the creation of the works and therefore cannot be an author.

PLAINTIFF's ATTORNEY: Objection. A tree drops its pine cones on its own initiative after the pine cones release their pollen or seeds, not in response to the wind.

SOLICITOR GENERAL: That is not necessarily true if it was quite windy that day.

JUDGE: That is a question of fact for the jury. Motion to dismiss denied as to the second work.

PLAINTIFF's ATTORNEY: While we believe that the Plaintiff is the sole author of the third work, it seems that we have the same question of fact as to the wind's involvement.

JUDGE: Correct. Motion to dismiss also denied as to the third work. Jury trial is set for the 13th of next month, right here in this courtroom. Court adjourned.

SOLICITOR GENERAL: I think I have tickets for a string quartet on that date.

JUDGE: Too bad, I guess you will just have to miss it. Look at the bright side. You will be able to hear Mozart's Concerto for Flute and Harp in D Major from the barn.

(*The* SOLICITOR GENERAL *looks at his wrist for the time*)

SOLICITOR GENERAL: Where is my watch?

BAILIFF: In your pocket.

(*The* SOLICITOR GENERAL *takes the Patek Philippe from his pocket, fastens it to his wrist and looks at the time*)

SOLICITOR GENERAL: It's five fifteen.

BAILIFF: I have five fourteen.

SOLICITOR GENERAL: What difference does it make? I have already missed the five o'clock train to Washington.

JUDGE: There is a milk train leaves at ten p.m. if you do not mind several stops, or we could find you a motel room near the station. By the way, do not forget to return the dunce cap to the Bailiff.

(*The* SOLICITOR GENERAL *hands the dunce cap to the* BAILIFF, *who drops it and shakes his hand*)

BAILIFF: There's bird shit on the dunce cap.

JUDGE (to SOLICITOR GENERAL): Counsellor, you will have to pay for cleaning. That will be five dollars.

SOLICITOR GENERAL: Let me give you a check.

(He reaches in one pocket after another and comes up empty each time)

SOLICITOR GENERAL (continuing): Sorry, Your Excellency, but I do not seem to have my checkbook on me.

JUDGE: No problem. You can give the Court some collateral.

BAILIFF: What about one of those expensive shoes?

SOLICITOR GENERAL: How am I supposed to walk in a cow pasture with one shoe?

JUDGE: Good point. Your watch will do.

SOLICITOR GENERAL: A Patek Philippe, for a lousy five-dollar cleaning bill? That's ridiculous.

JUDGE: Not to this Court. You can get it back at the trial, if you remember to bring the five dollars.

(*He motions to the BAILIFF, who approaches the* SOLICITOR GENERAL. *The* SOLICITOR GENERAL *holds his right hand over the watch, and they struggle until the* BAILIFF *removes the Patek Philippe from the* SOLICITOR GENERAL *and puts it on his own wrist*)

SOLICITOR GENERAL (to JUDGE): You're not going to let him wear it, are you? It must be kept in a safe place.

JUDGE: Not to worry. I'll keep it in my sight at all times.

(*He holds out his hand. The* BAILIFF *takes off the watch and hands it to the* JUDGE, *who after removing his own watch replaces it with the Patek Philippe*)

JUDGE (to SOLICITOR GENERAL): You can borrow mine.

(*The* SOLICITOR GENERAL *turns away and stomps off across the cow pasture in his expensive shoes*)

THE END

Also by Richard Heagy

Bad Grammar and Brass Monkeys
How to improve your bloody grammar and writing skills

ISBN – 13:978-0-692-76825-9
ASIN: B01KRYAL4I (e-book)

Practical advice and easy reading to improve your grammar and writing skills, with loads of examples and a dose of humour thrown in here and there.